MW01470642

In Recovery:
RISING
FROM THE
RUINS

Stories of Restoration and Resilience

Presented by

MICHELE IRBY JOHNSON

In Recovery: Rising from the Ruins
Stories of Restoration and Resilience

Copyright © 2021 by Michele Irby Johnson

All rights reserved. No part of this book may be used or reproduced by any means, graphic, electronic or mechanical, including photocopying, recording, taping or by any information storage retrieval system without the written permission of the publisher except in the case of brief quotations embodied in critical articles and reviews.

One Kingdom Publishing books may be ordered through booksellers or by contacting:

Michele Irby Johnson
www.iam-mij.com
www.onekingdompublishing.com
(301) 453-4770

Because of the dynamic nature of the internet, any web address or links contained in this book may have changed since publication and may no longer be valid. The views expressed in this work are solely those of the author and do not necessarily reflect the views of the publisher, and the publisher hereby disclaims any responsibility for them.

Any people depicted in stock imagery provided by SPJ Graphics are models, and such images are being used for illustrative purposes only.

Certain stock imagery © SPJ Graphics

ISBN: 978-1-7367296-1-8

Printed in the United States of America

IN RECOVERY:
RISING
FROM THE
RUINS

Copyright © 2021 by Michele Irby Johnson. All rights reserved.

Table of Contents

Co-Author Dedications

Dr. Lesia Banks

Dedicated to those who stretched my vision and didn't try to choke my dream. All connections "really do matter!!"

Alejandro Canady

Giving first Honor to my Lord and Savior Jesus Christ. I dedicate this book to my mother, Maedene Theus, for always believing, encouraging, and supporting me without judgement or criticism. She always reminded me from my youth to adulthood to always keep the Lord first in my life and there would be nothing that I cannot accomplish. I also want to dedicate this book to my sublime wife, Candice (Carlie)...Your love and unselfish sacrifices help me become who I am today. To you both, I love and thank you.

Kacey Cunningham

I dedicate this book to my mother, whom by an example of her life, has shown and taught me love, strength, and sacrifice. As her daughter, I have seen her outstanding growth in her faith walk, which has been a testament to my daily stride to be a better person, mother, and daughter. God has shown and taught me unconditional "spiritual" love, while my mother has taught and shown me unconditional "earthly" love, and for that I thank and love you! You are to me what I aspire to be for Jazelle. Thank you!

Oona Early

I dedicate this book to my husband who has observed me endure a lot of life's obstacles. The support he gives has been a tremendous blessing to me. He has watched me overcome so many challenges. His unfailing love has pulled me through some very dark times. I am so grateful to have him in my life. Thank you to my husband, Ernest, for always being there when I needed you most.

Hartford Hough

I would like to dedicate this chapter to the memory of my dear grandmother who faced death like the quiet warrior that she was. She showed me that death was simply a transitional phase that we must all face as we journey onto a greater side of glory from this life here. Also, to every pet parent who has lost a beloved animal companion... Know that the love you received from them is forever and embedded in your hearts. That love will never die.

Djuna Yvette Hunter

I am forever grateful to my Lord and Savior Jesus Christ. His faithfulness towards me continues to amaze me! He has been with me every step of the way through life's ups and downs. Even when I have not always been faithful in my walk with Him, He continues to show me His great love. To my most precious blessings, my children: Dominic, Hunter, Gabrielle, Hope-Elizabeth and Amelia-Grace, it is my prayer that through my story you will find understanding, compassion, empathy, peace, healing and the forgiveness that I have found on my healing journey.

Lakisha Jenkins

I dedicate this book to my deceased son, Keyshaun Mason. The day I lost him was the hardest day of my life. Keyshaun's smile could light up a room. He was adored by some and known by many. Losing him has caused me to push towards establishing purpose. Living life without him has taught me to value the things that matter the most. I'm certain Keyshaun is proud of my effort and strength. I will forever continue to strive pass the pain to become the best woman I can be. Keyshaun is my motivation to never give up or doubt my capabilities of succeeding towards my destiny. I will always love him. He is indeed my angel. Missing him constantly, Keyshaun Mason aka 'lil sway!'

Shaun P. Johnson, Sr.

I dedicate this book to my mother, Ava E. Tate, for her unwavering love and support towards me through the challenging times in my life. She knew what I experienced. Thank you, Mom! I love you!

Avery Kinney

To my wife, Iris, for pushing me, pulling me, and positively positioning me to be a better man. To my mother, Carolyn Foulks, for listening to my heart and loving me unconditionally. To my eldest and only blood brother, Aaron, who is in Heaven now and my sister, Adrienne, for putting up with me and fighting for me when I started the fight. To my children, Jayla and Avery, Jr., for teaching me all the cool things to say to make sure their dad is still relevant.

Julie Riley

I was blessed to witness my child give life to both of her own children and my world was forever changed. Grandchildren are a blessing from God. They own my heart and are the loves of my life. I want them to always know, when I am no longer on this earth, I will live on in their hearts and I will forever watch over them. I pray as you grow, you find true love; when you make mistakes, learn from them and do better; be grateful for your blessings and always be strong enough to forgive. Love, MawMaw.

Deborah Robinson

This book is dedicated to my loving husband, Bishop Nathaniel, for standing by my side in all my endeavors. My loving children William, Valencia, Raymond, Teron, Princess, and grandchildren that were there through all my highs and lows. The Jackson family, which had an impact on growing up in a neighborhood that had unconditional love. The neighborhood in Seat Pleasant, Booker T Homes, and Holland Garden is a place that it takes a village. Thank you for believing in my talents and gifting and not giving up on me.

Pastor Timothy Russell

I dedicate this book to my sister, Jamesetta Russell, for always being there during the highs and lows of my life. You stood beside me in my defeats and helped raise my hands in my victories while loving me along the way. You prayed and fought for me and I will be forever grateful. Let's continue to rise together!

Forward

I first met Michele Irby Johnson, a Chaplain Assistant at the annual DC Air National Guard Prayer Breakfast many years ago. As the Deputy State Chaplain for the DC Army National Guard, I was excited to be the preacher for the "Air Side" morning chapel service. The service was spirit-filled and meaningful to all military personnel present.

We were formally introduced by her unit chaplain. As the worship leader and organizer of the command worship service she needed no introduction. She loved her personnel. She worshipped, sang, and praised her God! Michele ministered not because of her military position and rank but clearly, she loved the Lord with all her heart.

We began to talk and share about the goodness of the Lord. We immediately hit it off like two home girls from the same hometown. We would reconnect at various military and civilian conferences, revivals, and ceremonies. We could talk for hours like the saints closing out the parking lot after a powerful Sunday service.

One would never imagine that Michele is a victor over domestic violence. She fearlessly accepted the grace and the love of God to walk a healing pathway to wholeness. On the journey, she discovered and re-discovered who God created her to be before the foundation of the world.

This book will reveal to anyone who is courageous enough to hear and listen with their hearts to these stories the backside of what you are going through. These co-authors were tested, broken, and delivered so they could minister to you. They each learned to declare in the hard places that God never leaves us or forsakes God's own.

Oftentimes, the pain that trips us up in the ruins cries louder than the peace and the promise of God. Our heavenly Father is always with us even when we do not remember God is still there. The ruins blind us into thinking that suffering is our lot. Rising from the ruins requires us to believe again that the challenges of this life will help to shape us into the person God created us to be. Rising implies coming up out of something that has held us down. We must rise again and again!

Through my own journey, I have discovered that the journey from ruin to rising is an intentional, fearless, and determined slow walk so I do not miss any lessons along the way. Every scar I have is a reminder that I once was wounded by life, others, and even myself.

During seasons of recovery, those mental, spiritual, and physical wounds began to heal, and the fading scars reminded me that wholeness was my portion! Some scars never fully go away less we fall back into the same ruins that held us captive. Like the fading of our scars, trouble really does not last always. I promise!

Michele Irby Johnson is proof that we can rise from the ruins! I have watched her life over the years with amazement and joy. She is a living epistle that should be read! My friend is soaring, prospering, and becoming a household name. Every co-author's story brings victory to life!

Learn resilience! Be restored! Rise up! I did... again!

Apostle Andrea Beaden Foster, M. Div.
Organizer, Another Chance Assembly
Retired Deputy State Chaplain (Major)
D.C. Army National Guard

In Recovery: Rising From the Ruins

Introduction

Michele Irby Johnson, Visionary
Speaker | Trainer | Consultant | Coach
Published Author | Talk Show Host | Pastor

Life can be tricky and sometimes it can be a little cruel! What do I mean? I mean there are times when what you desired, wanted, prayed for, was offered, or was promised shows up and turns out to be quite the opposite of what you expected. There are times in life when the unthinkable, the undesirable, the uncomfortable, and even the unforeseeable lands in your lap without warning and you are unsure as to how to navigate that reality.

Whether this life experience reveals itself at a young age or as you have matured, the experience has left an indelible impression on you emotionally, mentally, spiritually, financially, relationally, or physically. As a result, you feel as if you will wear the scars of your experiences forever; and the weight of them has had such an adverse effect on you that you are unable to see the light at the end of the tunnel. It is important to understand that everyone, at some point, has encountered some degree of struggle, disappointment, pain, rejection, abuse, emotional or mental distress, and the like. The truth is that life becomes a web of victories and defeats that take you on a journey that you would like to soon forget.

Take my personal story, for instance…

"Within the Ropes…In God's Hands!"
Michele Irby Johnson

"For it was not an enemy that reproached me; then I could have borne it: neither was it he that hated me that did magnify himself against me; then I would have hid myself from him: But it was thou, a man mine equal, my guide, and mine acquaintance. We took sweet counsel together, and walked unto the house of God in company." (Psalm 55:12-14)

There is nothing like being in the fight of your life, especially when you played some part in it. My story begins when I was struggling with being single after a divorce and trying to live my life as God intended. This was one of those life experiences that I did not see coming entirely. I was in a season in my life when I had no dating prospects years after my divorce…There was no one in particular interested in me as a single mother with a young son. I would often find myself asking God, "Why doesn't anyone love me?" Is there anyone who wanted me? Looking back, I realize those were very destructive questions. They were questions that would ultimately land me within the ropes of a fight that I could not possibly win on my own.

Have you ever asked God for something and you ended up regretting it? Yes, I found myself in a proverbial boxing ring fighting for my life rather than in the safety of a healthy, loving relationship that I desired. I allowed myself to be captivated by the lure of what I thought was a love that would take care of me... a love that would see me as a person with feelings, with a heart, with dreams and aspirations...a love that would do me no harm. Admittedly, I lowered my standards to become someone's significant other. I allowed myself to get into the ring with someone so that I could be part of "a couple." I wanted to be like others that I saw...those who *appeared* to be happy and in love. I wanted to belong to someone, and they belong to me. I wanted to have the security of a tangible relationship (not the one that I often fantasized about) that secured me and that was sanctioned by God.

I thought I understood what it meant to follow the commands of God, but I found myself compromising my faith to be in a romantic relationship. Desperation took a front seat and discernment took the seat at the rear of an extremely long passenger train. I pushed it as far away as possible thinking that accessing it would be more difficult if I kept it at a considerable distance. To my chagrin, I needed discernment more than I cared to admit.

So, here I was lonely and longing for love and when this six-foot four-inch gentleman steps into my office lighting my life up with his winning smile. To me, he appeared to be just what I was looking for… He appeared to be what I needed at the time. He was charming, funny, and was extremely attentive from our first meeting. He asked if he could borrow some of my cassette tapes (this tells you how long ago this was). I was so drawn in by his charm that I gave him the cassettes and immediately accepted his invitation to dinner. Who would have thought that I would be exchanging cassette tapes for my faith, my commitment to God, and ultimately my life?

He and I quickly became inseparable. In retrospect, it all happened too quickly. I was so enamored by his presence, his attention, his closeness, his concern for my safety, and his wanting to know my whereabouts at all times, that I ignorantly overlooked the beginning stages of power and control. What started as a whirlwind love affair quickly turned into something undesired. Before long, I began to experience the subtle coercive control actions of intimidation, jealousy, demeaning words, and jeering stares, which he justified as love. The mental, emotional, and verbal abuse then followed, but I excused his behavior as something that would eventually pass, and we would be just fine.

The first instance of physical abuse occurred when I went to his apartment and told him that I did not think that this relationship was going to work out. I realized that I did not like the controlling aspect of his love. He responded by shoving me to the ground and kicking me. In terror, I pleaded with him, apologizing, and saying that I did not mean it. Instead of him hearing my plea, he dragged me to the window, pushed the top half of my body through the window (he lived on the 11th floor) as he placed the knife to my throat. He said if he could not have me, no one could have me. I screamed and thanked God there was a knock on the door. He released me to answer the door. In his brief absence, I was able to get myself together. I grabbed my purse and ran.

I returned to work and confidentially shared the incident with my supervisor. I was so visibly shaken that she told me to go home and relax. After a week apart from him and a trip out of town, I was constantly being barraged by his calls. I finally answered and agreed to let him talk it out. He was relentlessly apologetic. He cried. He begged. He told me how much he loved me and that he would never do anything like that again. During a church revival, I clearly heard God tell me to leave him alone, but out of fear of being alone, desperation, and dare I say, stupidity, I ignored what I heard and eventually married this man.

Guess what? He lied and I fell for it! Throughout the marriage, I experienced every form of abuse at his hands, to include repeated spousal rape, choking, nearly having my hands broken, beatings while I prayed, isolation, blame, threats to my life, my co-workers, and my livelihood. I felt like I was in the middle of a boxing ring with my arms tied and my wellbeing suppressed under his power. I fought within myself every day. I was going out of my mind. Whenever he wanted to "show me," he would send the boys outside and I was left alone exposed to his violent frenzy. With each physical assault that I experienced, God entered the room and caused something to distract this man from carrying out the unthinkable. I told God that if He saved me from this mess that I caused, I would NEVER be so desperate to choose my flesh over my faith again.

It took me being in this situation to relate to what I have only heard about or saw in the movies. I endured an abusive relationship thinking I could change him...Thinking he needed me... Thinking I deserved the abuse or believing that the children needed us to stay together... Thinking no one understands and asking what will people say if they found out? I was in a caustic prison daily. When I moved, he moved. Where I went, he went. I was losing myself. I was living in a tornadic reality with no apparent means of escape. With every encounter at this man's hands, God's hands were protecting me from impending death or irreparable damage. One day God's loving hands provided the unexpected opportunity for me to escape, and I never looked back.

While living within the ropes, you do not readily find the strength to leave. You make excuses for the abuse and you try to convince yourself that he did not mean it until you see your life pass before your eyes on a regular basis. Beyond the abuse itself, there came a time that I had to see my own value and the truth of God's love for me. I had to come to the realization that my life is worth more than any love outside of the love God has for me. Exchanging my self-worth for the notion of being in love was no longer an option. Twenty-two years ago, I chose ME over counterfeit love. I chose God's plan and purpose over my desires and dreams and have found my value and my voice and now understand the consequences of every choice that I make.

Many women in abusive relationships are not so fortunate to escape their abuser. Since my escape from my abusive marriage, it has been my life's passion to help women to thrive after they survive their domestic violence ordeal. My lived experience postured me to become a transformational coach to walk women from a place of violence to a place of victory. Helping women to see their lives outside of the violence has its own reward. Although I participated in the mess, God's hands led me out of a place of pain and into a place of empowerment, strength, courage, resilience, and tenacity.

You have lived it and you survived it…Now what? You do as the old adage says… *'take lemons and make lemonade!'* You take the lessons you have learned, and you grow. While the situation may not have been favorable at the time, the evidence of what you confronted are the battle wounds of restoration and resilience. Yes, you made it to the other side of some of the most incredibly horrid ordeals you could have ever imagined. But here is the blessing, if you will... Your trials have become a testimony and your testimony becomes a landing place for others to know that they are not alone...they are not the only one who has been wounded by life, and they, too, can make it and thrive in spite of the upheavals of life.

Enjoy these heartfelt testimonies...stories of restoration and resilience... and allow them to be the springboard for your healing and entrance into a greater perspective on what you have been through or what you are going through so that you, too, can RISE! #Restored #Resilent

Time to Rise...

Michele Irby Johnson

In Recovery: Rising From the Ruins

A WALK IN THE PARK

Dr. Lesia M. Banks

Everyone has a Story. Some call it, baggage; others call it coincidence, and even some call it, destiny. Regardless of how it is labeled, our story – our past, is the preparation and training ground for our future. I Corinthians 10:13 says, *"No test or temptation that comes your way is beyond the course of what others have had to face. All you need to remember is that God will never let you down; He'll never let you be pushed past your limit; He'll always be there to help you come through it"* (The Message Translation). He will provide a way out so that you can endure it.

One of my favorite songs is The Crabb Family's *Through The Fire*, which proclaims: He never promised that the cross would not get heavy and the hill would not be hard to climb; He never offered our victories without fighting; But He said help would always come in time; Just remember when you're standing in the valley of decision and the adversary says give in; Just hold on, our Lord will show up…I am living proof that God showed up and fashioned me to survive. What do I mean by fashioned? Every storm that I had been through (self-hatred, which led to consummate low self-esteem, sexual molestation, and domestic abuse) – before being diagnosed with cancer – those storms, were simply articles of clothing, articles of armor, i.e., another shield that God equipped me with so that I could be prepared to stand up to cancer and fight the battle. The late Daryl Coley's song, *He Is Preparing Me*, simply states: He's preparing me for something I cannot handle right now; He's making me ready just because He cares; He's providing me with what I'll need to carry out the next matter in my life.

So, in hindsight, I thank God for the low self-esteem, sexual molestation, the domestic abuse, because all of that was just one more layer of clothing, one more layer of armor, that made my story, fighting cancer, seem like a *Walk In The Park*!!!! He prepared me to carry out the next matter in my life, He fashioned me to survive. By the time I was diagnosed with cancer, I was fully clothed...fully protected; I had on the whole armor of God, as described in Ephesians 6:11, to be able to fight that devil: Cancer.

TD Jakes said, "There is nothing quite like trouble to bring out your true identity. If you have agonized on bended knees, praying at the altar to know the purpose, and will of God for your life, and His answer does not line up with your circumstances then call it what God calls it. The doctor might call it cancer, but if God calls it healed, then call it what God calls it. Whatever He says, you are! We are to look the [story] in the eye without guilt or timidity and declare, *I have not come clothed in the vesture of my past. Nor will I use the opinions of this world for my defense. No, I am far wiser through the things I have suffered. Therefore, I have come in my Father's Name. He has anointed my head, counseled my fears, and taught me who I am. I am covered by His anointing, comforted by His presence, and kept by His auspicious Grace. I was called for such a time as this, and I have come in my Father's Name!"*

On May 19, 2009, I lay on a radiologist's table and as she conducted a single needle breast biopsy procedure, she asked the question: "Do you want me to wait and call you when you return from your trip?" Her tone and demeanor made me ask, "it's not good, is it?" Well, if you are asking me if I *think* it is cancer then the answer is yes. I lay there, my heart beating rapidly for a few moments. She asked if I wanted her to call someone. I told her no. I slowly got up from the examination table and got dressed; went outside the facility and sat down and begin to cry for a few minutes. I started to walk to my car and decided in that very moment that I did not have time to cry, but rather it was time to exercise my faith and once again internalize my personal mantra: "I refuse to be defeated." I may bend, but I will not break!"

Two days later, on May 21, 2009, I had been expecting to hear from the radiologist regarding the results of the biopsy. I was believing God that the lump was actually water, as the initial doctor had expected, and not anything more extreme as the radiologist had surmised. When the phone rang, I nervously answered it and the radiologist asked, "Are you in the car and do you need to pull over."

At this point, I already knew that she was calling to confirm her suspicion that it was indeed cancer. She was very blunt and nonchalant and just stated that, "we got the results back and yes, its cancer; I have already contacted the surgeon and you have an appointment for next Thursday, May 28, 2009. I asked her if it was treatable, she responded without a care in the world, "well everything is treatable, if it is caught in time."

I went into the bathroom and began to cry as I showered for dinner…afraid in that moment to touch that cancerous lump that had invaded my body without permission, without warning, and without announcing itself.

During my visit to the surgeon's office, he explained that it was Stage 2 and that I would need to have a lumpectomy and radiation and, that I should consider chemotherapy as a full body treatment plan in the event that the cancer had not remained localized to the breast. He went on to say, if cancer can ever be defined as good, that I had the best case as it was easy to treat, due to the location of the lump and my overall outstanding health.

I later read that the type of cancer that I had was Invasive Ductal Carcinoma. Just 20 years prior to my diagnosis, this diagnosis was grim, and the prognosis was even worse. Just 10 years prior a drug, Herceptin, had been identified to successfully treat estrogen positive breast cancer and at the time of my diagnosis it was the most treatable form of breast cancer. But God! I was called for such a time as this…

Look at God! Just a few months prior to the diagnosis and to me finding the lump, I had fasted during the season of Lent. I lost 34 pounds and happily went from a size 14 to a size 10 (and had even purchased one size-8 skirt, albeit stretchable… but a size-8 is a size-8; stretchable or not)!!! Lent was from late February to Easter Sunday. I gave up all meat, white products, and desserts. Being from the south, on Easter Sunday I decided that I would celebrate the end of Lent by eating the traditional southern meal, but something – obviously, the Lord – whispered in my spirit and said, "Don't go back to eating that stuff."

The next Sunday, I was out on my deck and gently scratched the top of my breast assuming that perhaps the detergent used on my sports bra had irritated my skin, instead I felt a huge lump and ran into the house, stripping to look in the mirror. The lump was so big I began to think something had just bit me, but my skin was not broken nor irritated on the surface.

I was 43 when diagnosed and had faithfully had a mammogram every year since the age of 35. Never received any indication that a lump was growing in my breast. Apparently, it was there for years, slowly growing, but hidden underneath the cover of fatty breast tissue.

The lump was growing with a desire and purpose to defeat me. I refused to call it *my* lump because it was not. It took up temporary residence in my body, but when I learned it was there, I spoke to the demon that it was and told it that I refuse to be defeated and I will not be defeated by something that is 2.5 centimeters, which is large in terms of a cancerous lump, but it was small and insignificant in size to the God I serve…my declaration…Cancer You Have Got To Go!

I often ponder that if God had not allowed me to successfully lose so much weight (after many previous unsuccessful attempts) that cancer could have remained in my body to the point where any possible treatment would have come too late. I was called for such a time as this… As I prayed about my situation and the treatment plan that lay ahead, God reminded me of the Theologian Reinhold Niebuhr's prayer:

God grant me the serenity to accept
the things I cannot change,
the courage to change the things that I can,
and the wisdom to know the difference.

I "accepted" the cancer diagnosis. It was here and it was not going to leave unless I fought it. I gathered the "courage" to have surgery, receive chemo (because God said nothing that I have made is unclean although the skeptics refer to chemo as poison); and, I had the "wisdom" to know that God was building up a story of UNBREAKABLENESS in me.

Instead of allowing the bitter cup of cancer to pass from me, God gave me the opportunity to drink of the cup because He knew that I would give Him the glory and constantly tell others about His grace and His mercy…that He is Jehovah-Ropha, God our Healer. John 11:4 reminded me that *"This sickness is not unto death, but for the glory of God, that the Son of God might be glorified thereby."*

I had never had surgery before and for me comprehending having surgery was more difficult than accepting the fact that I had been diagnosed with cancer. So, I went to the Word and was drawn to Psalm 91… *"He shall give his angels charge over thee to keep thee in all thy ways…"* I read it constantly and asked God to provide me with a peace that *"passeth all understanding."* The peace that is described in Philippians 4:7…and He did.

The confirmation of peace came as I walked into the hospital for surgery at 5:30am on Friday, July 10, 2009. As I approached the entrance to the hospital, I began to become sick to the stomach and I said I cannot do this. I went into the vestibule restroom and had a one-on-one with God. I prayed and I cried, and I prayed some more, and God clearly spoke to me and said, "I have granted you serenity, courage, and wisdom…per your petition… now be at peace and know that I am Jehovah-Ropha, your Healer!!" From that moment on, I fought cancer like it had never been fought before. I had surgery on Friday and was cleaning my powder room on Sunday… It had to be presentable for guests. I walked five miles almost every day while on chemotherapy and radiation. When my poor-intentioned boss told me that I looked sick, I used her *poor-taste* comments to motivate me to move forward and put on higher heels, shorter skirts, fabulous hair, and make-up to boot. I refused to be defeated and I refused to let her words cripple me. On the mornings when I felt a little queasy, I walked around the inner circumference of my house and prayed until I felt better; I jumped in the car and headed to the office. I was not going to sit at home and sulk and let cancer win.

During every one of the eight rounds of chemotherapy, I was dressed as if I was going to an event with make-up and matching head scarfs. I refused to be defeated and sit in that chair and look sick. Instead, I was conducting conference calls and surfing the web, while the chemo dripped into my veins for eight solid hours, every other Friday for four months straight. All the while, I spoke health into my life and walked into my continued health.

There is a verse in the *Through the Fire* song that says, "He never offered victories without fighting." My fight was a lumpectomy, a drug port inserted into my lower collar area, eight rounds of six to eight-hour chemotherapy sessions, one day of pre-chemo drugs, three days of post-chemo drugs for every round of chemo, 52 rounds of biotherapy, 56 sessions of radiation, and a daily dose of Tamoxifen for eight years. You cannot expect VICTORY, if you don't fight!

Through my treatment plan, I never got sick once, never threw up, never missed a day of work other than for day-long chemo sessions, and I still walked five miles a day most days. How in world could I have done that, you ask? My response, I didn't…God did. He prepared me for a *Walk In The Park*!

During speaking engagements, in daily living, and during devotions, I often recite and ponder on these words from The Crabb Family's *Through the Fire*:

"So many times, I've questioned certain circumstances

Things I could not understand

Many times in trials, weakness blurs my vision

Then my frustration gets so out of hand

It's then I am reminded I've never been forsaken

I've never had to stand the test alone

As I look at all the victories the spirit rises up in me

And it's through the fire my weakness is made strong"

A walk in the park is exercise and exercise makes you stronger. Breast Cancer, my "Walk in the Park," exercised my faith and it made me stronger, more resilient, and created in me a new mantra: *I Refuse To Be Defeated*!

The breast cancer battle reassured me that I have never been forsaken, neither have I ever had to stand the test alone. When challenges come, I use the memory of the breast cancer journey to constantly reassure myself that if God kept me through breast cancer, through molestation, and domestic violence, there is nothing that He cannot do. I no longer allow the menial things in life to weigh heavily on me: the opinions of people, particularly those who do not even know me, but are willing to provide a negative opinion of me; or a toxic work environment where supervisors and peers alike try to decipher my story without knowing any specifics, or even worse creating their own story about me; nor the constant bickering of family, friends, and/or acquaintances. These things no longer burden me.

Fighting cancer gave me an entirely new perspective on life. I now know what is important and what is not. I am no longer easily burdened by the things I cannot change; instead, I focus on living a life pleasing to God. I focus on living a life that entails sharing my story in hopes that it can help someone over a current or perhaps the unbeknownst next hurdle in their life. I focus on living a life of giving back to family, friends, strangers, and the community at large because so much has been given to me; life, health, peace. The tangible and intangible.

On April 8, 2017, during my visit with my Oncologist, he advised that after eight years of taking a daily dose of the drug Tamoxifen, I could now stop taking the drug and he voiced the words that will forever be branded in my memory "You are cured of breast cancer!!!!"

On May 19, 2021, I celebrated my 12th Post-cancer Birthday. I did not ask God for a remission, but rather for a healing because He is Jehovah-Ropha, God our Healer. My message to you is that God is not a respecter of persons and whatever He did for me He can and will do for you. Keep the faith, be encouraged, speak life, and refuse to be defeated!

LESIA M. BANKS, Ed.D.

A Survivor and Strategist who thrives on
CreatingCareerConnections™.

Dr. Banks is the Founder and CEO of Dr. Lesia M. Banks Enterprises, LLC, a career coaching, and organizational development consulting practice and is a certified Global Career Development Facilitator. Her coaching focus: career pathways, doctoral dissertation, and small business development. She is a thought partner and consultant in organizational leadership theories and practical implementation.

Dr. Banks has more than 30 years of Federal government experience to include serving in various leadership positions in numerous Executive Branch Departments. Her responsibilities have encompassed the entire spectrum of Human Capital management, information access law, audits, and internal review. She has led diverse staffs and managed multi-million-dollar budgets. She served as a Technical Coach for President Obama's Youth CareerConnect Federal Grant Initiative, a Dissertation Committee member at Capella University as Visiting Scholar and at Grand Canyon University as Content Expert.

Dr. Banks has authored two books:

C^3 CreatingCareerConnections   (A   Pre-College   to   Career Enrichment Guide)

All Connections Matter: Change Your Circumstances by Changing Your Connections (An A-to-Z Guide to Checking Your Connections Are They Stretching Your Vision or Choking Your Dream)?

Dr. Banks holds a MBA and a Doctor of Education in Organizational Leadership with an emphasis in Conflict Resolution. Dr. Banks is a 2012 Harvard University Fellow and recently completed the Women's Leadership Executive Education Program at the Yale University School of Business. To learn more about Dr. Banks, visit www.drlesiabanks.org.

BREAKING FREE FROM THE BABYSITTER

Shaun P. Johnson, Sr.

I was born in 1972 at Cafritz Memorial Hospital now United Medical Center in Southeast Washington, DC. I grew up in the projects called Valley Green. The Valley Green complex had three sections – first court, second court, and third court. I, my mother, stepfather, and sister lived in the first court. After my mother moved us from a one-bedroom apartment, we upgraded to a two-bedroom apartment in the next building. I remember the Candy Lady, the Giant Food, the Ice Cream Truck, playing tag with friends, parties, fights, alcohol, and of course, drugs. If the projects of Good Times had a baby with the projects of New Jack City, it would be Valley Green. For me, there were good times and bad times. One of my family members sent me a black and white picture of three young black children standing in front of the building I used to live in. As I looked at the picture, I started reflecting on the memories and how God helped me to break free from the babysitter.

I was five years old, and my Sister was two years old. I was enjoying life and loved watching Saturday morning cartoons while eating a big bowl of Captain Crunch cereal. At the time, my mother received a monthly government check and food stamps. My mother and stepfather would go out to parties and cabarets. They were living it up. There were many times that I noticed they were not living it up. While arguing and fussing, my stepfather was abusive to my mother. It was an unhealthy environment, and I was too young to understand what was going on. Most of time, I would close my eyes and cover my ears in my room wishing it would stop. I hated him. In his rage and anger, my stepfather would take his anger out on me and beat me until I turned black and blue. He beat me so bad that my butt was bleeding. I barely could sit down. I was a young boy growing up in an abusive home and I was stuck in the middle of their mess.

My mother and stepfather were searching for a babysitter and they found one in the building where we used to live. Her name was Judy. In the hood, they called her, *"Judy with the Big Booty."* Judy was dark skinned and twenty-five years old at the time. I would not say that Judy was pretty, but she was a straight up freak who was feigning for young boys and girls. To me, Judy was scary. She even had a smell that reeked of sin. Judy had an older brother and two parents who were deaf living in the same apartment. It felt like a nightmare every time I had to stay with Judy, the babysitter. It was not bad at the beginning, but it took a turn for the worse. Because of the darkness of the apartment, I did not want to eat their food, sit on their furniture, or go to sleep. I was scared. I just wanted to protect my sister. I did not want to be there. At five-years old, I was not stupid. I was smart. My mother raised me right. I could spot trouble from a mile away and the babysitter was big trouble.

Judy was touching and rubbing me on the living room couch in front her deaf parents. Her father and mother kept watching television ignoring us like they were used to it. They let her do it. I was Judy's next victim. With a loud scream, I said, *"Stop. Leave me alone."* *"You are mine,"* Judy replied. On another day, it was just me and Judy. Her parents and brother were not home. My sister was not with me. When I was alone with Judy, I was afraid and terrified. I knew something was not right. Judy told me to come to her room. She said, *"I need you to take off your clothes and stand in front of me."* She kissed me on the lips and said, *"Do you like that?"* I shook my head and said, *"no."* Then, Judy gently caressed my young body with her hands. She grabbed my butt and squeezed it. Judy said, *"Are you okay?"* I said, *"What are you doing? I do not like this. Stop!"* She said, *"It is okay. Stay calm. Just follow my lead."* After she caressed my young body with her hands, Judy started feeling my young male part. Judy told me to get on the bed and she started sucking my young male part. When she was done, I took off running down the hallway naked in a state of confusion. It was like I was in the Twilight Zone. As always, Judy was determined and she said, *"Calm down and come back to the room with me. I will not hurt you. I love you and I want you to love me!"*

I came back to the room with her. Then, it happened! I am standing in front Judy naked. There was so much going on in my head. If I give in, she might leave me alone. Judy said, *"You are so cute to be five."* Then, she said, *"Kiss me on my lips!"* I kissed her on the lips. Judy said, *"Kiss me on my neck!"* I kissed her on the neck. Her moans sounded like what I heard when my mother and stepfather were in their bedroom. Weird! Judy said, *"Now suck my breast!"* I sucked on her breast. After sucking on her breast, Judy kept moaning, she said, *"Eat my "lady parts!"* She said, *"Let me say it another way so you will understand. Eat me! This right here!"* On the bed, Judy lifted her legs and spread them as far as east is from the west. Judy said, *"Do you like what you see?"* I just nodded my head and waited to see what was next. My heart was racing. *"Now taste me,"* she said. Judy grabbed the back of my head and pulled me closer to her girly part. She said, *"Take your tongue and lick me good!"* I started licking her. She was moaning and pushing my face into her *"what in the gushy world is going on"* lady parts. Judy kept calling my name saying, *"Is it good, Shaun?"* I was already moving my head up and down as I questioned myself. It took some time, and I was tired. It kept going and going. I am saying to myself, *"When is this going to end?"*

Judy told me to get on top and have sex with her. *"What is sex?"* I questioned. She grabbed my butt and guided my body. I could not fight her off because Judy's legs were wrapped around me. After *"sex,"* Judy wanted me to go back to "having a meal." This entire session went on for about an hour. It felt longer than that. Judy started screaming and shaking. With intensity, she grabbed my head. When Judy was finished, there was a calm that came over her. While still laying between her legs, I looked up at her with my sticky and smelly face and said, *"Can I stop now?"* Judy said, *"Yes. You can stop. You know how to do it to me. I want it like this every time you come over. Do you understand?"* I thought it was over. On another day, Judy was watching me and my sister. We were all in her bed. I was facing the wall. My sister was in the middle. Judy close to the door. Then, her brother came in the room. I looked and he was naked. Judy's brother got in the bed and they started having sex. I was uncomfortable. I could not get any closer to the wall. Judy reached over and started touching me. They were yelling at me saying, *"Get over here. Turn around."* I grabbed my sleeping sister and ran out of the apartment. They did not come after us. I guess they kept on having sex. What do you call it when a brother and sister have sex? Oh…incest! What is insect? *"No Shaun. Not insect. Incest,"* as one of my family members shared with me.

Many times, I tried to tell my mother and stepfather that Judy was touching me inappropriately. They did not believe me. My parents approached Judy and she lied. After the encounters, I cried and told my parents again. They finally believed me, and I never returned to Judy's apartment. Judy could no longer do what she did to me. At the time, I was traumatized. I was quiet. I did not want to go outside. It felt dark and lonely. At five-years ago, I was introduced to sex. I learned later in life that it was molestation. Molestation means *"sexual assault or abuse of a person and the action of pestering or harassing someone in an aggressive or persistent manner."* Judy was a babysitter who molested me. She forced herself on me, made unwanted and improper sexual advances, and took total advantage of me. All the signs where there, but I was too young to see it. I did not have a desire to be with girls. At one point, I questioned my sexuality. Am I gay or straight? At the time, my doctor gave me a physical and examined my young male part and said, *"Protect it and you are not gay."* This experience opened me up to pornography and masturbation. I felt it was safe for me to do because I was afraid to have sex with girls and get a disease like AIDS. I never saw a Therapist or a Counselor to help me with this childhood trauma.

At age seven, I accepted Jesus Christ as my Lord and Savior. I went to church with my cousins. I loved staying with them on the weekends. Their home and church were a place of safety. It was my haven from the hell in the hood. As I grew in my faith and continued to be a scholar in school, I guess the pain of the past left me. No more trauma. No more wounds. No more Judy. No more stepfather. He left. My mother was overprotective and tried to keep me out of harm's way. One day, I went to Judy's apartment. She was surprised to see me. Judy looked bad from years of using drugs. At the door, I said to Judy, *"I forgive you. Jesus loves you. Take care."* In that moment, I felt a release. I was strong enough in my faith to make the choice to forgive. We must forgive ourselves for being hurt and to forgive those who have hurt us. I never saw Judy again. It reached a point when my mother said, *"Enough is enough!"* Before we moved, I learned that Judy drowned her baby boy in a scorching tub of water. She was arrested and later died in prison. Her big brother was arrested for selling drugs and he went to prison as well. He was later killed. It was a sad and tragic end for them both.

When I look back, God saved me, and He spared me. His grace was on my life. I often wonder how many boys and girls Judy molested. How many grew up in the ruins of the hood and never recovered? I can say that I was blessed to break free from the babysitter. I recovered. Today, I help others who struggle with sexual addition by sharing how I overcame the residue of my experience after being molested by the babysitter. Now, I can share my story and tell people that they can rise from ruins of molestation.

I have learned a great deal from being a victim of molestation to becoming a survivor. When I look back over my life, I survived that situation. Former Secretary of State Hillary Clinton quoted, *"Every survivor of sexual assault deserves to be heard, believed, and supported."* There is no telling what the babysitter would have done to me, but I survived it. As a survivor, you must speak your truth. It

21

is your story. When I speak my truth and tell my story, I do not look for sympathy or attention. I am not the victim. I do not play the victim. I am a survivor. You are a survivor. We must set the world on fire with our truth. We never know who needs to hear our truth. As blessed and favored as I am, I do not have to worry about guilt and shame from being sexually violated. The Apostle Paul stated in Galatians 5:1, *"It is for freedom that Christ has set us free. Stand firm, then, and do not be encumbered one more by a yoke of slavery."* The babysitter was a yoke of slavery. Because I have freedom in Christ, I do not feel hopeless or worthless. I have hope and I know my worth. I was not a mistake. I am a miracle.

After I picked up the pieces and put my life back together, I could not be silenced. Dr. Martin Luther King, Jr. said, *"Our lives begin to end the day we are silent about things that matter."* My life matters to someone who needs to hear. Today, I share my story with boys, girls, men, and women about molestation and I desire to start a movement to bring awareness to the subject. When God restores, He repositions you to reach people. I was in a dark and confused place, but I knew I was a shining light in this world to show compassion anywhere, to anybody. I will find a way to do something good and help others.

I believe my experience has helped me to be the Christian man I am today. I could not let my past define me. I am defined by who God has destined me to be. While I have had my share of struggles, sufferings, trials, and tribulations, I am determined and driven to continue to fulfill the purpose in my life. I hope the words in this book have tugged at the heart strings of the reader, captivated the depth of the soul, and convinced their minds and spirit. This is a real and serious issue especially in the African American community. It is a pandemic called molestation and men and women molesters, rapists, and abusers need to be committed or convicted. I hope I have expressed my deepest emotions and have enlightened those who will find the courage to transform the world with their own stories. Do not be afraid to tell your story. Inspire and impact lives. Change starts with you.

SHAUN PATRICK JOHNSON, SR., D.MIN

Dr. Shaun Patrick Johnson, Sr. was born and raised in Washington, DC. He accepted Jesus Christ as his Lord and Savior at the age of seven. Shaun is an honors graduate of the District of Columbia Public School System. He studied Graphic Design and Communication at the University of the District of Columbia in Washington, DC and graduated with an Associate of Arts degree. He was called and licensed a Minister at the age of nineteen, ordained and licensed an Elder at the age of thirty-five, and consecrated and affirmed an Apostle at the age of forty.

Shaun received a Doctor of Ministry Degree with a specialization in Pastoral Leadership and Care from Hope Bible Institute and Theological Seminary in Fort Washington, Maryland. An apostle in the Lord's Church, he is the Founder and President of Apostolic Grace Evangelistic Fellowship, LLC *"winning souls for God's Kingdom."* He has been a Professional Freelance Graphic Designer of SPJ Graphic Designs, Inc. for over 23 years and a Professional DJ for over 30 years. Shaun is the Host of Get Right with God TV Official on YouTube and Get Right with God Radio Broadcast on Sensational Sounds Radio. He is happily married to Michele Irby Johnson. Together, they are the proud parents of three sons, Shaun

Jr., Matthew (Angelina), Jordan, one daughter, LaShaun and one grandson, Cameron. Connect with him by:

Email: drshaunpjsr@gmail.com
Website: www.shaunjohnsonministries.com
Follow him on FB/IG/TW @drshaunpjsr.

CAN I HAVE MY HEART BACK: THE FIGHT TO BE WHOLE AGAIN

Timothy Russell

The encounter at the garage...

It was a normal summer day in Foster City. It was hot with a slight breeze, so the heat was manageable. I decided to ride my bike over to the baseball field to see some of my friends play in their games. I stayed for a while but decided to head home for some reason. Oh, how I wish I would have stayed at the baseball field.

When I got home, I saw my dad going from the upstairs room to the garage with boxes. He was startled to see me and kind of stuttered when I asked him what he was doing. You have to know that my dad was my hero...period. He was everything I wanted to be, and I was proud to be his son. He had a presence about him that demanded respect, but he was a gentle giant. Organized, a leader of women and men, a success story are just some of the ways I would describe him. I always looked at him in awe.

He told me that he and my mom were having a difficult time getting along and he was going to leave for a short time so they could work it out. I had no clue what he was talking about because at 12 years old I had never been in a relationship to understand what I know now as a man. I trusted his words because I had no reason not to trust him.

I stood at the garage and watched him drive away. I waved and stayed there until I could no longer see his car. I went back to doing what I normally do…being a 12-year-old boy. I did not realize being a boy would end that day because of the choices of my dad.

I didn't just lose my dad, I lost my mom, too…

When my mom and sister got home that evening, immediately my mom could tell something was wrong. She noticed some things missing and asked me where my dad was? I replied "Oh mom, I came home and saw dad putting things in his car. I asked him what he was doing, and he said, he needed to leave so you all could work some things out."

My mom looked at me with shock that quickly turned to disgust. She asked me, "you let him leave?" and it was at that moment I knew I made a mistake and failed my mom. My sister looked at me in shock and knew I was in major trouble. I believe from that day until the day my mom died, she blamed me in some way for not 'holding the line' until she got home. It did not help that I looked like a young version of my dad, so every day she looked at me and probably saw her 'stupid' son that looked like the man that abandoned her. Her nightly tears in her room were like knives piercing my heart and I found myself not asking for anything from her and walking on eggshells. I spent the rest of my childhood and teenage years between the space of "just trying to be a kid growing to be a young man."

I realize that on that summer day my heart stopped beating for me and only beat to the drum of trying desperately to have my mom forgive me and love me. My heart was broken, and I cried silent tears. As we moved from location to location finally settling in a studio…yes four of us in one room… all I could do was stare at four walls that became mirrors of my failure.

As I grew in size and my ability to play sports, I would always look into the stands for my heart to walk in and start beating again. I hung my hopes and dreams on my dad keeping his word to me and coming back. I was too young to understand adult relationships and the details of a broken marriage. I know now that I and my siblings were casualties of a broken home, but as a child I felt worthless and disregarded. My sister once told me that one day my dad came home, and I held onto his leg and begged him to stay. She said I kept saying "please, for me, please," but even those words were not enough to fix what was broken in him and in my mom. I did not know so; all I did was become more and more choked out by what I thought was abandonment and rejection.

In my senior year of high school, the athletic and academic scholarships came pouring in, but I struggled with leaving my mom like my dad had done years ago. I abandoned my dreams of attending the school of my dreams to stay close to home and to continue to be the man my dad walked away from being for my mom. I put my plans on hold to make up for what I felt was my terrible blunder at 12 years old.

Time to unpack this luggage...

My young adult years were a blur. All I remember was living in fear of the next great moment of abandonment and rejection. After all, at 12 years old I was loveable and innocent and the person I loved the most walked away from me; so why would anyone want to stay with a scarred young man who had lost all of his innocence.

For about 10 years, I was functionally depressed, and no one could help me...especially the church, where I had spent so many hours and days. I grew more and more angry destroying everything in my path. I did not want anyone to touch me or get close to me. One day I took a walk with Jesus...alone! I poured out my heart and to my surprise, I found out that He really did love me and cared about the pain and the reality of it. I realized I knew how to worship. I knew how to sing praises. I knew how to prepare and deliver powerful sermons, but I never unpacked the pain of abandonment and rejection planted in my life at 12 years old. What I had was a major issue that only God can heal, but abandonment and rejection had me afraid to open up to anyone...even God.

Issues are birthed when the seed of unrighteousness is conceived in our lives. In my case, the seed was trauma caused by my parents. It definitely was not intentional because I believe they loved me, but their decisions became a gateway for the issues that plagued me for years.

One thing I know to be true, the devil has invested time and energy into knowing what makes us tick. Remember, he is our adversary and is seeking to devour the children of God and he seeks to do this by working through our issues. Issues are areas of our lives where there has been a track record of past failings. In addition, these are areas that we are seeking, fasting, and praying to be delivered through the power of Jesus Christ.

Every child of God has issues in their lives that cause them to live beneath the privilege and joy God intends for us to live in. Without His help and strength, these areas we would constantly befall us. Look at this promise in Jude 1:24, *"Now unto Him (God) who is able to keep us from falling (consumed by our issues) and present us faultless (righteous) before the presence of His glory with exceeding joy..."*

As I mentioned earlier, once the seed of unrighteousness is conceived then what is birthed is issues. Issues are reminders used by the devil as weapons of condemnation...Reminders that constantly challenge our position with and in God. If the devil can get us to doubt who we are in Christ Jesus, then he has effectively affected our relationship with our Father.

Back to the garage...

Part of my unpacking process was going back to the very place of my worst hurt and let me tell you…it was painful. I could not understand why God would have me go back to this place where I lost my heart. Was He punishing me for what I did in my relationships or with my kids? Whatever it was, I did not feel like this was helpful; but I trusted God with everything, so painfully I obeyed.

He instructed me to build an altar of worship in my darkest place. I screamed and cried like the 12-year-old boy who was traumatized. It felt good to go back and live for a moment in the childhood I was robbed of on that summer day. I was already forgiven by God, but I had not forgiven myself for everything that was the product of my trauma.

One thing I learned through this process is that the altar of defeat becomes your altar of victory when you surrender it to God. Don't get me wrong, the process was ugly. It was yanking scabs off unleaded wounds where there was major infection. I realize now that things that are done to us affect us, but if they are not dealt with in a healthy way then what has affected us will begin to infect us.

It's crazy because I kept telling myself I was alone again, but I kept hearing a voice calling out to me saying "You are not alone!" I felt guilty, but I kept hearing "You are forgiven!" I felt death would be better than to deal with the shame of so many mistakes, but I kept hearing "You will live and not die!" The most important thing I kept hearing was "You are loved!" With one deep breath I could breathe again and feel my heart coming back to life. Finally, I was living and not just existing!

The Healer...

Now-a-days, I spend countless hours ministering to those, like me, who have experienced some trauma, but never unpacked it. One of my favorite stories in the Bible is when Jesus said to the man at Bethesda, "Do you want to be WHOLE?" I see myself as that man in so many ways; laying there for so many years wanting someone to help me. Like the man, I had so many excuses for why I was still laying there wallowing in my pity and abandonment. But just like that man, I had an encounter with The Healer. He set me free and gave me back my heart.

Don't get me wrong, I am not perfect and never will be, BUT I serve a perfect God Who is perfecting me daily. Teaching me how to love. Teaching me how to forgive. Teaching me how to live whole in Him...the blessed life full of His glory and blessings.

My mom passed away 13 years ago, and I am glad her pain and declining health challenges came to an end. I believe she is resting in the bosom of Jesus. My dad and I have a restored relationship and I love him. We do not talk about that summer day because I would rather just spend the rest of our days on this earth enjoying one another. I spend many hours and moments in the garage. It is a place of healing for me. My sanctuary. Who would have thought that would ever happen, but with God all things are possible!

I learned that nothing the enemy speaks into and around my life can supersede what God has spoken over my life. In addition, I learned that God meets us in the valley (our low places) and does not just wait until we climb the mountain and declare victory. He literally is our climbing partner.

Through my restoration, I have used the process the Lord brought me through as an education for others. I realized the process can be ugly, but it does not mean that God is not working it out. My hope is to encourage others to stay in God's plan of redemption and restoration for their lives.

I hope that every reader understands that they can be made whole. No matter what the situation or circumstance or addiction or brokenness is...God is bigger than it! And our purpose, His purpose for our lives, is greater than our issues. It is time to break out of our "houses" of despair and touch the hem of His garment.

My ordeal became my testimony of God's deliverance. I am a walking and living miracle. God's love met me where I was and brought me up and out. The process was ugly, but the outcome is that I have been made whole through the power of God, through Jesus Christ. He truly was wounded for my transgression and bruised for my iniquities.

PASTOR TIMOTHY RUSSELL

Timothy Russell is the Senior Pastor of New Hope Christian Fellowship, located in Hayward, California. With over 30 years in ministry, his passion centers around helping individuals find and walk in their designed purpose. Timothy is the author of *Conquer or Be Conquered* and is currently working on a book project entitled *Rising from the Ashes*, which details his journey of overcoming functional depression.

Timothy is married to Vanessa Russell and together they have seven children, five adult kids and two teenagers still at home. Their lives are dedicated to their ministry, their family, and the communities they serve.

To learn more about Timothy's ministry and work, visit:
www.nhcfonline.org
https://www.facebook.com/hope4hayward

FROM GRIEF TO BELIEF

Oona Early

Psalm 118:17-18 in the Message Bible says *"I didn't die. I lived! And now I'm telling the world what God did. God tested me, he pushed me hard, but he didn't hand me over to Death"* (The Message Translation). This scripture has been my testimony! I can relate to this passage of scripture because I have experienced a lot in my life, but I am still here to testify to the world of God's goodness. Yes, I have been tested, but I am living to say it is only by His grace that I'm alive and well.

Growing up, I was raised in a one-parent home...raised by my beloved grandmother, the late Mrs. Ethel Mae Moore Roberts. At the age of 4-years old, my mother left me to relocate to the city for a better life. So, for years I grew up trying to figure out why I was left behind. I grew up with a void of love. My grandmother reared me very strictly. I could not do what some of the other girls my age was doing. I could not hang out late. There was no sleeping over friend's houses either. I did not understand it then, but I am grateful now for my upbringing. As I got older, I realized my grandmother was only teaching me what she was taught. I can truly say my beloved grandmother lived a long life of gratitude. I have seen her take $20.00 and stretch it the whole week. She was a woman of strength and many talents. She did not have a lot of education, but she knew how to overcome life's obstacles. She was excellent with her hands and was known in the community for her works. She could bake, cook, upholster, sew, and she was a helper to others.

My grandmother passed away in 1997, a few years before I gave my life to the Lord; but I often wondered what life would have been like if my beloved grandmother had lived longer. Would the life I now have make her proud? She was my mother and my father... She was the only foundation I knew. But when she passed, my life – as I knew it – turned upside down quickly. I can remember her telling me for so many years, "Oona, ya better learn how to do and what to do because muh ain't gon be witcha always." And sure enough, that day came, and my beloved grandmother and caregiver took her last breath right in front of me. My life turned for the worse that day. I tried to cry it out. Work it out. Pray it out. But I was really grief-stricken. I went down a road of deep dark depression. No one seemed to be able to understand what I was dealing with. I suffered breakdowns. Family was nowhere to be found. Everyone went their separate ways. It was not that the family could not be there; it was that they chose not to be there for each other.

Grandma was like the glue that held us all together and the pain of losing her had me in and out of the hospitals. On medication after medication. I was on some type of medication that was so strong that I could not keep my saliva in my mouth. There were times I could not sleep. I would be up for days at a time. I did not have an appetite. My life now was unbearable. I was thinking how I would make it without my grandmother. The pain of losing her was unreal. I had no one to talk to about what I was dealing with. I was going from house to house. Living with different people from the church. I had to take my relationship with God to another level. I cried out to Him. I asked Him to heal me inwardly.

It took me years to get over my grandmother's death to the point that I could function. I could not maintain a living anymore after her death. I could not function. I lost my home. I lost my car. I only had the clothes that I could get out of my home. Prior to my grandmother's death, I was a thriving cosmetologist and a worship leader. I hosted my own ministry on local TV called "Healing Begins Within," which God gave me shortly after my grandmother passed. God let me know that some things have to be birthed through pain; and that sometimes, something has to die so that something else can live. But after her death, I no longer found interest in any of my talents, gifts, and capabilities. Singing was a strong passion, even writing songs was one of my heart's desires, but nothing could prepare me for what I would have to endure. No one, but God!

I can remember asking God, "how long would I have to deal with the pain, the grief, the depression, the family betrayal?" But even after the family betrayal, God used my Pastor at the time – the honorable Bishop Randy B. Royal (deceased) and the Philippi Church – to make a huge impact in my life by blessing me in more ways than one. Bishop Royal used his expertise to help me along my way by providing me with somewhere to live, with food, furniture, and so much more. They stepped right in just in the nick of time. I met Bishop Royal through a well-known preacher in the community and soon after I joined the church body and began to work faithfully for well over 20 years under Bishop Royal's leadership.

I can truly say that my faith in God and having such an outstanding pastor and church family has gotten me this far. Because even when my natural family turned away, God had a ram in the bush. I have learned that people come, and people go, but God remains faithful. I still had my ups and downs, but I remained steadfast in God and stayed under my pastor's wings and developed even more.

Through my shortcomings, I have learned to take the bitter with the sweet…to not dwell on past failures, but to allow them to be my teacher for my future. I have learned to take the good with the bad...to walk by faith and not by sight…to always put my trust in God and not in man…to never lean to my own understanding, but in all my ways acknowledge Him and He will direct my path. Through it all, I can truly say that some people may have left, but God remained true to His Word. He said He will never leave us nor forsake us. As a result, I got to know Him in a more real and personal way.

I have seen physician after physician, and they have all had an opinion as to what I may have been going through. I have listened to many of them, but I have often wondered why they had a direct timeline as to when a person is supposed to be grieving. They have said that you are only supposed to grief a certain period of time. But my question to those who write these guidelines was, "What have you gone through?" "Who have you lost close to you?" Grief and depression are real, but so is God. And although it took me many years to be able to cope with my grandmother's death, God has truly shown Himself mighty in my life. It has been hard, but I am a living testimony as to what much prayer, fasting, and praise looks like. People can only speculate, but until you have actually been down this path and have seen how God can take a disaster and turn it into a testimony, you'll never be able to understand or to relate. Now I would be lying if I say I do not have times where I cry and miss my grandmother, because the truth is that I miss her right now...I just know that she is no longer suffering, and she is in a much better place. I am at peace with that.

You may ask me, "How did you make it through this far?" and my response would be, it was nobody, but God. I praised God and I prayed. I read my Word and got to know God in a more intimate way. I can now say that I know Him to be a mind-regulator because through it all He is still healing me. So, yes, Psalm 118:17-18 is still very real to me because when friends and family thought I would never recover, God, with His good self, showed up and rectified every situation. He proved Himself mighty in my life. He made ways when there seemed to be no way. He said, *"I am the Way, the Truth, and the Light."*

My advice to you would be to trust God with everything – even when it seems dark and dreary. Trust that He knows what we need and when we need it. As the song writer said, "My good days outweigh my bad days…I won't complain."

Throughout my ordeal, I had to have therapy because depression was taking a toll on me physically, mentally, and socially. I want to encourage you to understand there is nothing wrong with going to therapy. The practical side of our faith is to pray and use the means of what is available to us to ensure that we can walk in total healing and wholeness. Sometimes you need to talk things through in order to be able to be productive. God does all things well and there are times when He will allow the collaboration of our pain to get us to His purpose in our lives.

By going through the process of my healing, I learned that healing is a continuous process; and that through my process, I have grown into a better, more mature woman in ways I could once only imagine. My purpose is more prevalent now that I have allowed my past experiences to be my teacher by learning from it. Through my relationship with God, I learned to trust and rely on Him and not on mankind. I have also learned that everyone goes through challenges – some more severe than others – but during my process, I have been strengthened where I once was undeveloped and immature. I learned that I was barely functioning and not making an impact. Through some of the choices I made, it caused more pain than the actual healing that needed to transpire.

By using the pieces of my life that have been restored, I have used it as a testament to help other damaged, scared, and hurting women. During the grieving process, I dealt with the cycle of looking for love in others as a way of escape from the pain I was currently feeling. I went through bad relationships and bad counsel in hopes of easing the pain. By going through my ordeal, I have developed more compassion and empathy for people who are going through depression or grief. I have learned that my past did not destroy who God has called me to be in life because we often think our past can hold us up from being who we are destined to be.

My prayer is that individual lives will be transformed, renewed, restored, and developed; and that every word read will come to life and help put their broken pieces back together again. I have come to realize that without my past I would not have this opportunity from God in the way that I presently do. I know Him to be my Healer. I know Him to be my mind regulator. I know Him to be my shelter in the time of a storm. So, without my past experiences, I would not have this growth and development.

I used to trust in the fact that people would be there for me, but as I got older, I began to see that people were not always going to be there. I had to get to know God in a more personal and intimate way. Life has taught me that when you are doing well and on the top of the mountain, people will cheer you on and be by your side; but once you start to go through some things in life, sometimes people will stand back far away from you. They fail to understand that God will allow you to go through some things to get you closer to Him. He wants a relationship with us, not just weekend visits. He wants total custody, and He wants to abide inside each of us. I know that He came that we might have life and life more abundantly. I am happy to live life more abundantly with fullness of joy and peace. I have not arrived. I am still a work in progress. God is still working on me; but I am so glad I am not where I used to be. I am changing. I am going from Grief to Belief!

OONA EARLY

Oona C. Early is a wife, mother, cosmetologist, Pastor, and a disabled veteran. She is a powerful and anointed young lady with a testimony of deliverance, break-through, healing and ultimate victory! She is an effective witness to many as to what the power of prayer can do. One of her favorite scriptures is *"Delight thyself in the Lord and he will give you the desires of your heart"* (Psalms 37:4). Oona is a gifted psalmist, composer, and playwriter for the Lord.

She faithfully served under the dynamic leadership of the late Bishop Randy B. Royal for over 20 years. While there, she actively participated and served as Praise & Worship Leader, Door-to-Door Outreach Ministries along with many other activities. Oona Early has a passion for God's heart. She has a deep commitment to serve God's people with excellence. The initial birthing of her ministry began on WOOW radio station then to MRE Network after the death of her grandmother, the late Mrs. Ethel Mae Moore Roberts.

On September 3, 2013, Oona entered into marriage with Pastor Ernest R. Early. In God's time and season, this union has birthed Tower of Fire Ministries in Raleigh, NC. With this divine move with a Kingdom assignment on her mind, she sees God's hand opening doors and allowing her gifts and talents to be used to the Glory of God. In a spirit of expectation, she awaits to see the manifestation of the Lord for such a time as this!

I'VE BEEN THROUGH HELL
NOW I'M ON FIRE!

Avery D. Kinney, Sr.

My life literally caught on fire back in 2004! I began to experience what I call a "HELL BREAK OUT!" A hell breakout is when Hell breaks out in more than one area of your life – all at the same time. My marriage was failing. My ministry was failing. My health was failing. My secular career was failing. I had a decision to make while my life was on fire! I did not want to STOP, DROP and ROLL like they taught us to do when there is a fire because FOR ME, that would mean STOPPING my life, DROPPING my responsibilities, and ROLLING around on the floor like I was in a padded cell feeling sorry for myself. I made a choice to make the most of it and so it became a season of critical training for me.

Every fiery situation, every problem, every conflict, every loss, every disappointment, and everything that burnt me in the process, I decided those experiences contributed to my time of critical training. God was using the fires that I was trying to put out – initially in my own strength – to refine me. He was using the fire to process me for His promises for my life. For a minute, I lost my mind! I did not go to church...my flesh was OUT OF CONTROL...folks had stopped asking me to come and preach...I was a secret alcoholic…I was addicted to pain pills…and was living in my car. I did not have anyone to blame, but myself! When your life is on fire, it is not the time to quit on life and start acting a fool. It is a time to survive and ultimately to thrive. It is a time of testing, but it is an open-book examination.

I learned that everything that I was going through was basic training for everything I was going to. God was using that season to move me from maintenance to manifestation! After every fire there is always some maintenance that must be done. The private rooms of my life were being swept out on a public platform. That was so humiliating! The humiliation stirred up the manifestation of greater clarity concerning my life, a greater anointing because of the crushing and the things God began to cancel out in my life. I experienced a greater manifestation of self-esteem and self-worth because life left me feeling worthless. I discovered that I came from a lineage of people that revealed that 'bounce back' was buried in my DNA. I found out that fire will cause things that have been buried alive to cause your burnout to become a breakout.

God wanted to show me that when we are comfortable and life feels manageable, we delude ourselves into thinking we do not need God as much as we really need Him. Then something happens like my "Hell Breakout." You lose your job. You almost lose your mind. You discover your spouse's betrayal. You discover the disloyalty of friends and family members. You discover that your leader is a

Judas. You discover that Jezebel has a key to your house. The Hell Breakout was a time of discovery and sobering revelations.

To be honest, my life was on fire before it caught on fire because my heart was burning due to the absence of my father. My father was not my daddy. I know, it sounds complicated, and it is! In other words, my father was not a part of my life and upbringing. And as a result, I have spent most of my life wondering if I was good enough, living with feelings of inadequacies, feelings of rejection, and trying to fill the "daddy hole" that was filled with anger and fire by my father's absence. It wasn't until I was in my 30's that I had to make up in my mind that the hole in my heart wasn't going to rule my heart any longer. I had a few revelations in that Kairos moment (opportune time):

- Don't be led astray by what life has wounded you with.
- Pick yourself up and PUSH THROUGH!
- Remain open to learning new ways of being or journeying to places beyond your comfort zone.
- Seek clarity, do the work, embrace the process God has you in.
- Repeating cycles is NOT AN OPTION!
- What you learned – LEADING TO THIS SEASON – taught you how to live at a different level.
- If you are going to be great, you have to be consistent, even in questionable moments of life.
- Keep your heart, your habits, and your head right.
- Pursue your deliverance with enthusiasm.

Getting back to my first marriage… After several months of being married and attempting to play a role I was ill-equipped to fill,

I decided to stay because I was in it and I did not want to get a divorce. One morning I got in my car and drove around the Washington Capital Beltway until I finally ran out of gas. I refueled and kept driving for a few more hours. I was very unhappy. I was unhappy with myself. I was unhappy with the climate of my life. I was unhappy with feeling responsible for the happiness of my ex-wife. It took me a while to learn that pretending like a problem is not there, doesn't solve the problem, it only expands it.

Unfortunately, my marriage and my relationship with my wife's children became collateral damage of the baggage I brought to the marriage: the daddy issues I nursed, the hidden self-esteem issues, and my competing with my father-in-law for the honor and respect of a wife who did not know how to be who I needed her to be with me. MY HOUSE WAS ON FIRE and we were all being choked out by the smoke. I inflicted so much pain on myself and we were inflicting pain on each other because of OUR reckless choices. My wife and her children were hurt because I was loving them as a malfunctioning man. I was hurt because my ex-wife was a malfunctioning woman. Because of immaturity and trying to save face, it was difficult to see and accept back then. It took her abandoning me, while I was in the hospital having a stroke, to see myself. That was a huge price to pay, and I still regret the pain I caused myself, her and, her children. My failed marriage presented me with a few revelations:

- I should have focused on healing myself first before I ever attempted to love a wife and children.
- A failed marriage taught me the correct sequence of God's order for a marriage and ministry.
- Nobody can love you if you are not prepared to receive it.
- Be honest about your baggage – Do not hide it!
- Make God the priority in your marriage and not your family's opinions.
- Make God present in your marriage by being equally yoked.
- Make God the Protector of your marriage and not the efforts of flesh and blood.
- Make God permanent in your marriage by allowing Him to preside over it on the front end and not when it catches on fire.

The fire of life created many opportunities for me. I recall feelings of desperation. I had many decisions to make. I had some directions that the Lord was giving that I had to execute. It was a time of development. It was a time of determination and I dealt with many disappointments. They all built me to last through what the enemy meant to use to lay me out! The desperation I felt was causing my senses to shut down and was robbing me of the hope that things would ever change. I was blinded to possibilities and opportunities because fire creates blind spots. It literally forced me to rely on God's power. The decisions that I had to make made me a target for temptation. I had to rely on God's direction while I was being burned by life. The directional signs and signals from God saved my life. Even in the fire, God has a specific route for me to take!

God will use the fires of life to force you to reconsider and reassess God's will and direction and it will burn away your disobedience. One of my revelations in that season was that "disobedience reinforces a distorted sense of direction." I have found that character cannot be developed in disobedience and ease. Once I began to address the fires that were burning out of control in my life, I had to get a determination down in my heart to adjust to where God was taking me. In that process, my reoccurring issue was disappointment. For me, disappointment results when our expectation of something positive, profitable, pleasurable, or purposeful becomes overshadowed by the threat of it not happening. What I had to learn is not to allow my disappointments to become destructive to my life, but instead allow them to become instructional for my life. Disappointments become destructive when you allow them to consume you.

Meanwhile where is God? He was there all the time. Sometimes I could not feel Him, but He was there! The Holy Spirit was the Teacher. I was the student. The firefighter and life were the arsonist. I would like to share a few things I had to train myself to remember (memory is a powerful thing):

- Accept the fact that life is out of our control (things that matter the most to us in life are the things we control the very least and that can be frustrating).

- Remember who God is: *"For I am convinced that neither death nor life, neither angels nor demons, neither the present nor the future, nor any powers, neither height nor depth, nor anything else in all creation, will be able to separate us from the love of God that is in Christ Jesus our Lord."* (Romans 8:38-39)

- Take the risk of faith because the fires of life are risky. Take the risk of faith. The cost of faith is always a risk. No risk, no faith; it is that simple. The only way we can develop the confidence that what we believe about God is true, is to try Him out. I had to try God for myself! I could not walk on what my mother told me, what my pastor showed me, or what I heard on Christian television. I had to take the risk of faith in the fire of life.

- Do not face the fire alone! The Bible declares in Hebrews 10:24-25, *"Let us consider how we may spur one another on toward love and good deeds. Let us not give up meeting together, as some are in the habit of doing, but let us encourage one another--and all the more as you see the Day approaching."* God is our Ultimate Refuge, but there are times when the relationships on earth are a tangible place of safety in our lives. Pastor Michele Irby Johnson was a tangible place of safety for me when my marriage was on fire. I had been evicted and between jobs. Pastor Michele was one of God's Grace-based franchises on earth that God used to house me and nurse me back to my senses even in the midst of her putting out some fires in her own life! I am forever in her debt.

Always remember the attributes of God: God is Omnipresent and is everywhere. He is not restricted by location or distance. God is Omnipotent and is all powerful. There is nothing is too hard or impossible for God and with Him. God not only has power, but He is power. God is Omniscient and He knows everything. He knows how and why things happen. God does not need to study to acquire knowledge about you. He knew you would go through hell and that now you would be on fire and you will not even smell like smoke!

You may be wondering: How do I survive? How do I make it through? How do I live the life I feel destined to live after what I have survived, in the face of so many factors seemingly out of my control? You are not alone! I have pondered the exact same questions. I have sought answers, in the name of greater personal freedom and happiness, and I have made some discoveries. Some of us have been reacting to the events of our lives and responding to our expectations of what we thought should have happened! For me, it all came into focus when I examined my own life and the areas in which I was struggling, I asked myself if my expectations were contributing to my unhappiness. I had to get my expectations in check so that my life would stabilize. I knew that I wanted to live free, so freedom became my pursuit.

The Bible says, *"He who the son sets free is FREE INDEED!"* I wanted to get to my "free indeed!" Living free, isn't that what we all really want? Free from the burdens and stress of trying to live up to, or down to. I wanted to be free from the anxiety that I was not going to succeed in areas of my life. For you, living free may seem so far from your current reality that you are not sure it is even possible, or what it could entail, for that matter.

For way too long many of us have been giving our power away to life, people, circumstances, and situations. It is time to take your power back, which you do by making the commitment to live free and STAY FREE. As I have navigated many seasons of my life, I have seen a radical difference in my stress level, happiness, and overall disposition. Being at PEACE and living in PARTNERSHIP with staying free has helped me become more flexible and accepting of the processes in life, changes in my life that previously would have been upsetting and besetting.

The prophetic impact I want to speak into your life is to "GET READY TO RECEIVE new strategies and new strength!" As you seek the Lord of Breakthroughs and obey His instructions, your "Valley of Trouble" will become the very place where you have a fresh encounter with the One *"who always leads us in triumph"* (2 Corinthians 2:14). He will not only give you new strategies, but He will ALSO give you new strength to carry out those strategies (Isaiah 40:31). Do not get weary if your victory does not come right away, nor be discouraged if you encounter a difficult battle before your breakthrough. If you are struggling to shake off the memories of past failures, remember what God's Word says, *"Though the righteous fall seven times, they rise again"* (Proverbs 24:16 NIV). No matter how far, or how often, you may have fallen, the Lord will lift you up and give you victory!

AVERY D. KINNEY, SR.

Bishop Avery D. Kinney, Sr. is a native of Washington, DC and is a sought-after speaker, conference presenter and a two-time Blacks in Government workshop presenter. As a speaker, Bishop Kinney has shared messages in churches, town halls, convention centers, hotels, corporate venues, educational institutions, and correctional facilities.

Bishop Avery D. Kinney, Sr. is the author of "Sneak-A-Preach," the visionary behind The Leadership Boot Camp, Human Resources Consultant known as "TheHRman" and prophetic counsel to ministries and businesses across the country. Based in Richmond, VA, he currently operates as the Founder & CEO of The Prophet's Porch, which airs twice weekly on Facebook LIVE and on YouTube.

Bishop Kinney is a well-respected social media personality, and he utilizes his global platform to minister to people from all walks of life. He is the husband of Pastor Iris Kinney and the father of two and the grandfather of one.

To stay connected to Bishop Kinney and to experience his ministry, visit www.theactivationcenter.org as this is the online ministry hub of all things Bishop Avery Kinney. To book Bishop Kinney, he can be reached at info@theactivationcenter.org.

LESSONS LEARNED THE HARD WAY

Julie Riley

I was born on May 2, 1965 in Front Royal, Virginia to Patsy and Bill. My mother moved to Front Royal to live with a girlfriend to escape an emotionally, unhealthy home. Patsy was depressed and desperate to get out. In Front Royal, she was introduced to my father Bill. They fell in love and got married. About a year later, on May 2, 1965, Patsy gave birth to her first child, a daughter they named Julie. Patsy was 25 and Bill was 32. The marriage was volatile, and Bill was very abusive. She had threatened to leave many times, but he told her if she ever did, he would kill her.

She finally made the decision to leave, and we moved in with my grandmother. Bill went to my grandmother's looking for Patsy, but she was at work and when he knocked on the door and my grandmother saw it was him, she called the police. He broke in the apartment through the bedroom window and as he was walking out of the bedroom, the police arrived. Bill saw the police and took the gun he had hidden in his pants and shot himself. My mother came home and saw police cars and an ambulance and knew something was terribly wrong; she was about to find out how wrong. My father took his life in March of 1968. He was 35 years old. Although Bill was abusive, Patsy loved him deeply, and this tragic event would scar her for life.

About nine months after his death, my mother's friend set her up on yet another blind date hoping it would help her move on. They fell in love and were married on August 9, 1969. He had a career as a D.C. fireman, he treated her great, and he was good with me. He was what she needed. We moved out of my grandmother's apartment into a house in Riverdale, Maryland. My grandmother moved with us also. My mother gave birth to her second child, a boy on March 22, 1970. During my 5th birthday party my, baby brother had a seizure and had to be rushed to the hospital. My mom spent most of her time watching over my brother.

I was only five years old, and my life changed dramatically in a short period of time. I now had a man I called Dad, and although I knew he was not my "real" father, I never questioned it. I had a baby brother who was sick, and my mother now spent most of her time and energy on him. My stepdad worked shift work and was not home much and my grandmother worked full time. I was a quiet child by nature and never asked questions about anything that happened, as I did not want to upset my mother. I had and still have no recollection of my biological father, but I knew the man my mom just married was not my real father. This is the beginning of my feeling confused, lost, and afraid. No one seemed to notice or maybe I did not show it. I became very close to my grandmother, who I called Mamaw.

We had a very special bond. She was the one constant, loving, and stable adult in my life during this time and she would continue to be my source of stability and the one person who always showed unconditional love for me until the day she died. Our bond grew stronger through the years and I always knew, no matter what, she would always be there for me. I miss her to this day.

Fast forward to 1975, we moved to Waldorf, Maryland, and my grandmother moved to Virginia to be near her sisters. I started middle school the year we moved and then went onto high school. I did well in school, got good grades, it came easy for me. My brother struggled academically but excelled in sports. My mother continued to worry about my brother, my stepfather worked shifts and was not around much.

I started suffering with depression in my early teens. I have spotty memories of my childhood. I started rebelling around the age of 16. I had thought about killing myself a few times during my teens. I began drinking and going to parties every weekend; many times, coming in drunk as my mother sat there waiting for me, scared my father would wake up and find out. She never told him anything bad because she was afraid of how he would react.

So, I grew up in a home of secrets and lies, none of which was ever talked about. There was no arguing. When there was a problem, we just did not talk, and eventually acted like nothing happened. There was a complete lack of communication and very little affection. With no one paying much attention to what I did, it was easy to get away with a lot and I did. I graduated high school in 1983. I drank a lot with my friends, came home when I wanted, made up stories of where I was going, and no one questioned it. On the outside, I am sure I looked like a happy, normal teenager having fun with my friends, but on the inside, I felt broken, lost and, still invisible.

In October 1984, I found out I was pregnant by my boyfriend, who at the time was a year younger. He was the second boy I had sex with. He graduated high school in June of 1984. We married on December 1, 1984. My daughter was born May 9, 1985. I suffered from severe post-partum depression. To say the adjustment from one day being an immature kid with no responsibilities, no real parenting skills, no life skills, to having to be an adult, a wife and a mother was overwhelming, which does not begin to describe the way I felt.

The marriage fell apart when my daughter was about three years old. I moved into Section 8 housing and was basically a single parent, trying my best to support and raise this little girl on my own. I grew up on my own, and I did the best I could with the little I knew. I suffered from severe bouts of depression since my youth, always trying to hide it from everyone. I worked a full-time job for the Federal Government. I struggled financially. I was never taught about money or how to balance a checkbook and have always had trouble balancing my finances.

I was 23, still immature with no life tools, no real guidance or structure to draw from and I was a mess. I prayed to God every night that I would not wake up in the morning because I felt so guilty for not being a better mother to this beautiful little girl and maybe she would be better off with someone who could give her everything she deserved. I felt like a complete failure and was filled with unrelenting guilt. The truth is, I did not know how to be a mother. I was never taught or shown. I never had stable parents.

I was emotionally damaged and did not feel good about myself and did not feel worthy of anyone or anything good. People always seemed to like me, and they were good people, and I remember I could never understand why they liked me and felt if they really knew what a mess I was, the mistakes I had made, they would feel differently.

I got into relationships with a few real losers. They cheated on me, mentally and emotionally abused me; one was physically abusive and hurt me badly enough that I ended up in the hospital twice. Time and time again, I continued to let them back in my life, expecting things to be different. The very definition of insanity, doing something the same way over and over and expecting different results. At this point in my life, I felt like I was losing my mind. It felt like a cycle had been repeated.

I was able to escape the abusive relationship. I worked hard to get myself back and regain some self-respect and some self-esteem, but it took years. I believed I had worked through all my trauma and problems and came out on the other side a stronger person. I would soon find out that 'working through' and 'pushing down' were two different things.

I remarried at age 38 after only dating my husband for six months. I was at the top of my career and it felt like things were finally falling into place and I would live happily ever after. My daughter and my family adored him as did I. He was everything I needed at the time. We were happy for a few years until we started to grow apart. My happiness was short lived. I was going through another divorce, I was not doing well at my job and decided to take an early out and retire before I was fired. Our house was going into foreclosure. My daughter and I were having a lot of problems and I was back in a very familiar dark place. It was too much, and I was too tired to try again.

So, in September 2012, I attempted to kill myself, not a lame attempt, I truly wanted to die. Apparently, my neighbor came by because my dog was out and called 911. The ER pumped my stomach, and I spent the next seven days in a psych ward. I was still carrying a load of guilt and regret that was getting too heavy to carry.

I became addicted to prescription opioid pain pills towards the end of 2012. At first, they made me feel amazing. They numbed all the emotional pain. I did not feel depressed; actually, I did not feel anything and that was fine with me. The addiction advanced quickly and within a year, I was totally dependent on them. I got into a shady pain management clinic. Within a year, I was taking double the amount I was prescribed, so I had to buy them off the street. I was financially ruined. I was losing everything, and my life was a nightmare. Eventually, my daughter found out and told me if I did not get help, I would not be able to see my grandson until I did (he was 6-months old at the time).

That was my rock bottom, I lost everything that meant anything to me. I entered a 30-day program in California on December 26, 2014. Going to that center was the hardest, yet one of the most profound experiences of my life. I learned that sometimes good people make bad choices. I got clean there and have not used since. God had a different plan for me.

My daughter is 35, married and they have two beautiful children. I have acknowledged and apologized for my mistakes. I spend as much time with my grandchildren as I can, as they are my heart and I love them more than they will ever know. I see them often and we are close. I make sure they know how much I love them, and I pray someday my daughter will be able to move forward, forgive me, and we can have a better relationship. I have learned that is something I cannot control and pray every day that God will soften her heart.

By the grace of God and counseling, I have let go of the guilt and regret I could no longer carry. God has a purpose for me and loves me unconditionally. I am on a journey learning to forgive and love myself and I am not defined or judged by my mistakes. I believe God allowed me to endure some very hard situations for a reason. I learned from them and He showed me I was always stronger than I thought, and I am worthy of all the goodness this life has to offer. I pray my story will help someone see they are stronger than they know and just hold on, and trust God.

My journey has shown me that we all have a purpose in this life. Some of my worst nightmares were actually my biggest blessings. There is no better life teacher than experience. I came through some very difficult times, with no one showing me how to survive. It was a long, difficult journey and I came to a point when I did not think I could take anymore.

I turned to God and begged Him to show me what He wanted me to do. I needed to learn the lesson of believing in myself and I had to dig deep and know my worth so I could move forward to help others. I truly believe He had me go through the horror of domestic violence and drug addiction, so I can help others who may be struggling with these issues. Both situations have a stigma of shame and fear. Abused women stay with men and are afraid to leave and do not know where to go for help. Drug addiction is a disease and people need to be educated on this so the stigma can be removed so people feel safe to reach out for help without the fear of being judged and rejected.

I know without a doubt what God's purpose is for me and everything I have been through now makes sense and my calling is clear. People need to be educated on the subjects of abuse and addiction, as both of these subjects must come out of the dark and into the light where these issues can be discussed openly. There are women's shelters and organizations that can give them guidance on how to leave their abuser. People can recover from addiction with the help of treatment centers and a solid support system. Abuse and addiction affect millions of people and many times it is a matter of life or death.

I am not ashamed of my mistakes or bad decisions as those are what put me on my journey with God and finding the purpose He had planned for me. I pray my story will help someone know that there is a way out and there are places to go for help. I will help bring both of these problems to light and do whatever I can to help those who are struggling.

The judicial system has come a long way in dealing with domestic violence, but there is still a lot of work to do to make it easier and less fearful for those being abused to come forward. Drug addiction is a disease and a horrible epidemic and needs to be treated as such, allowing people to get the help they need, removing the shroud of shame and humiliation.

Looking back at all the hard times I experienced and made it through, has shown me I was never alone; God was with me every day, every step of the way and He never gave up on me and loves me through all the good and bad. He has shown me that I am enough!

JULIE RILEY

I'm **Julie Riley** and I am a single mother and a grandmother. I was born in Strausburg, Virginia and raised in Waldorf, Maryland. I have struggled with Major Clinical Depression Disorder since a young age as well as severe anxiety and panic disorders. I have suffered from overwhelming guilt, abandonment issues, PTSD and have self-sabotaged for decades. I am a survivor of Domestic Violence, which includes severe emotional and physical abuse that landed me in the hospital twice. I am also a suicide survivor.

In 2012, I became addicted to prescription pain medication. Initially, the pills helped dull my emotional pain, until they did not. The emotional numbness the pills provided did not last long until it turned into a total nightmare. I lost myself, my family, friends and was financially ruined. I entered into a recovery center in 2014 and have not used since and will continue to use the tools I learned there to never use again.

God continued to put me through some very difficult times until I finally got what He had been trying to show me. I am strong, I am worthy, and this life is worth living. I am now on a journey learning to love and respect myself and to fulfill the purpose God has for me. I believe He brought me through all of my struggles so that I can share my experiences with others and hopefully help even just one person make it through. To connect, I can be reached at julesbrown1965@gmail.com.

MY MISSING PIECE

Alejandro Canady

Growing up for me had its challenges. You never know how life will throw pitches to you until you stand and wait to see where the ball is going to go. Then at that time, you can choose to swing or wait for the next opportunity.

I grew up with my half-brother, Deon, raised by my mother and grandmother. The Lord blessed them to buy their first house in the Winter of 1972. I remember my Uncle Stanley temporarily stayed with us. My brother and I did not have our fathers to raise us. As for Deon, I felt he was truly fortunate to have the acknowledgement his dad gave him and that he knew where he came from. I was not so fortunate, and it created sibling rivalry and friction for me growing up. Although we had one of my uncles, Stanley, living with us, he was not what you would consider a role model for his nephews. He had his own life trying to find himself practicing the Muslim religion.

One day I remember walking towards the kitchen for something. My Uncle Stanley stopped me and said, "As-salaam alaykum." "Peace be upon you." He told me to respond back to him by saying the words, "Wa alaykumu s-salaam." Not having a clue of what my uncle's beliefs were, I honestly did not care to know about it. Later in life I understood that the Quran says: "When you are greeted with a greeting, greet in return with what is better than it, or (at least) return it equally" [al-Nisa' 4:86][5]. My mother and grandmother raised me up as a Christian. That is what I knew then and still to this day.

Another time my uncle wanted me to respond back, but I reluctantly refused. He became angry and snatched me up off the floor and took me into my mother's room to correct me. My mother was not home nor was my grandmother. As protective as they both were with both me and my brother, neither would not have let him spank us for such a minimal reason. He first put me on the bed and had my legs folded to a point where I could not move. He spanked me with a belt while telling me "What are you supposed to say to me?" I cried and told him "I was sorry" pleading to him to stop whooping me.

After several spanks, I told him the greeting he wanted me to say, and he stopped. I resented my uncle for what he did to me. He put my brother through the same thing when my brother either forgot to say it or did not want to say it, but at that time, my brother got whipped in the garage on the concrete floor. My brother also pleaded for him to stop. I was afraid to tell our parents what he had done to us. I do not think my brother ever did. Thank God my Uncle Stanley later moved out of the house and we were free of that bit of turmoil of our youth. He estranged himself from the family for years for reasons unknown.

One Summer, my brother received a call from his father wanting to see him. His dad lived in Wichita, Kansas. His dad would send for my brother to come and visit with him and his family there. I remember his dad would also occasionally send him money. I could only imagine how good that made him feel. At least, I felt my brother should have been happy to have his father in his life. Over the years as brothers would do, we fought and bickered. I remember he told me during a heated argument "You're just a bastard! You don't know who your daddy is." I thought to myself, "Wow, I really do not know who my daddy is."

In my teenage years, I had asked my mother, "Whatever happened to my dad?" She did not remember much about him. She would tell me, "I wonder whatever happened to Onnie "Ray" (my dad's name)?" She told me he was a singer (I didn't know if he sang professionally)," but I later found out he did. He also had worked as a warehouseman for Sears Roebuck. My mom suggested that if I talk to my Uncle Stanley, maybe he could tell me more about my dad. You see, my father and Uncle Stanley were friends first before my dad met my mom. Growing up I would hear, "Who's your daddy?" I did not have an answer and it made me feel odd not having a father in my life. Time would eventually answer my questions.

The year was 1991, my Uncle Rayfield (my mother's brother) was looking for my Uncle Stanley. Through several searches, he was able to locate him and a valid phone number. I asked Uncle Rayfield if I could have his phone number. Despite previous feelings I had with Uncle Stanley, I just wanted answers about my dad. I spoke to Uncle Stanley, who then relocated to New York City. I began asking him what he remembered about my father. He said that they met years ago in Berkeley, California and became friends.

During that time, my dad was introduced to my mother and a relationship later developed. Stanley confirmed that my dad did sing in a group and he had made a couple of 45 RPM records. After my own research of groups that he told me about, I found someone named Darryl Cannady from The Natural Four, but not Ray. Hmmm. My thoughts were, "could some letters from the name Darryl be switched around?"

Guys back in the day would give false names and I would not put it past anyone at this point. During this time, I was working at Price Club in Richmond, California. A co-worker there told me an old girl friend of hers dated a guy from the Natural Four. She was able to get me a contact to Darryl Cannady.

I received a call from Darryl. We met in Stockton, California. I told him the story about me and my mom, and I asked if he could be my father. He said he remembered my Uncle Stanley, but within limits because when I first met Darryl, he was a recovering substance user. I later met his daughter and two sons. Darryl and his daughter had their doubts, but they thought it might be possible that I could be Darryl's son because the lifestyle he had in the past. His sons embraced me, and I have been building a relationship with them all lasting over 16 years.

One day Darryl confessed his real feelings and told me he did not think he was my father. I had already changed the spelling of my last name to his and was accepted by his family and some of his friends. I started to feel wanted and loved, but that was a hard blow to my heart. I agreed to pay for a DNA test to settle any doubts he had. The results came back that we were not related. I was heartbroken. Darryl told me anyone would be proud to have me as their son. He said he would help me locate my real dad.

It was January 2007. I had searched the internet again and, on my search, God stepped in. I tried spelling my name without a letter. The last name on my birth certificate was spelled CANADAY. Darryl's name was spelled CANNADY. I retried the name without an N spelling it CANADY. That was it! It was always CANADY and his first name and middle name on my birth certificate was correct. I was in so much confusion for years, but clarity finally came that day. I saw my real dad's birthday; we were days and exactly 30 years apart in age. His name, address, date of birth, phone number was all right there. Finally, my questions were about to be answered after so many years of wondering.

On Sunday, January 27, 2007 after coming home from church with my mom, I told her I was going to call the new number I found on the internet. This was the very first time I would ever speak to my dad. I prayed and braced myself for any possibilities including accepting denial if that would happen. I called the number listed and a young boy answered. I asked him if I could speak to Mr. Canady. He said to hold on. A man says, "Hello!" I responded "Hi, Mr. Canady, my name is Rey and I live in California. I wanted to know if I could ask you some questions." He told me okay. I asked him did he ever lived in Berkeley, California and he responded, "Yes!" I asked him did he own a light-colored Pontiac Bonneville convertible, did he work in a warehouse, did he ever sing in a group, and did he know my Uncle Stanley? All his responds to me were, "Yes!!"

My heart is racing at this point. He told me him and my uncle both once applied for a post office job. My dad was accepted for the job but took on a warehouse position that paid more. I said, "Mr. Canady, I have been looking for my father for an awfully long time, and I believe that you might be him." He asked me, "what's your mother's name?" I told him and he said her name and said he remembered her. He then asked me for my phone number and my address. I gave it to him. He said I am going to send you some pictures of me and we will be in touch. I was good with that. He got off the phone and I told my mom, "I think I finally found my daddy." I just felt it. She said, "I hope you did. I hope for your sake you did."

It was true. I received calls from my new older sisters and a nephew. The mind-blowing part for me was when I finally got a picture of him when he sung with a gospel group Singing Angels of Hempstead, Long Island, New York. Talk about a spitting image! There was no denying it. My oldest sister Trivonda saw my graduation picture from high school and said, "Oh my God! He looks like me! That's my brother!" Later that year, I flew to New York for a family reunion and met daddy for the first time face-to-face; I met my sisters, a couple of nephews and, a few of my HUGE family members on the East Coast.

Everyone was so sweet, loving, and welcoming. My stepmother did not come and had major doubts and animosity towards me. It was not until after my dad's passing, I asked Trivonda if she would do a DNA test with me. She agreed even though we already knew the truth. This was done to simply put my stepmother's doubt to an end. It came back 99 percent we ARE RELATED! I felt it was totally unnecessary since my dad accepted me and, for the most part, owned up to it. He even told me, "Yeah, you look like me" with a chuckle. I believe he always knew, but he was scared. It did not matter to me. I found out the truth and I did not have any hatred towards my parents. It was what it was, and God brought me through it all.

We have so much love in our family today and I cherish the seven years and seven months that I had with my dad before he left this earth. I told him I loved him, I hugged and kissed him. He told me he loved me, too. I learned that even in such circumstances, God can bless you and turn things around in your favor if you just trust Him and let Him do it. If he could change my stepmother's heart from bitterness to love and acceptance, He can do it for any of you out there. Try God. I promise you will never be sorry.

What I have learned during my ordeal was to speak up for myself and not remain a victim to other people's issues. I cannot accept the responsibility of someone else's pain and anger and why life is not the way they think it is supposed to be. I cannot be afraid to speak my mind, my concerns, and feelings because no one will ever know what you are going through unless you voice what is on your mind. Suffering in silence should never be an option to anyone. I learned to love myself and to surround myself with people who know the meaning of the word love; my acceptance of imperfection within myself and with others without judgment. Growing up without a dad taught me several things.

1. Being true to myself. Do not put my family through the emotional pain I felt for years.

2. Accountability. Not blaming myself for my dad not being in my life and punishing my children behind it. I must and will rise to be the best father I can be with the help of the Lord to my children

who not only need it but deserve it. Also, keeping in mind that no child asks to come into this world. It is my decision and responsibility to have them, raise them, and teach them right from wrong.

3. Forgivingness. I forgave my father for not being in my life as a child and I forgive myself for not believing in myself.

My restoration. I discovered a new level of patience and understanding with others when I was in search of my father. I realize and accept the fact that life may not give you the results you expect from it, but it can bring necessities needed in order to move forward despite unfavorable outcomes that may be on the surface.

More importantly, I learned the importance of love and its powerful force. Once it is combined with forgivingness and understanding you have created a solid life foundation that is very fulfilling and totally unbreakable. The pieces of my life that are now restored are shared in love with my family and friends. By this, I mean giving my heart openly and reassuring hope to those who have been hurt, damaged, or broken by life's roads of the unexpected.

My hope is that my story brings you closure to any unanswered questions in your life; compassion and healing to the hearts of those who have doubted themselves, been ridiculed and hurt by others, including family members. Forgive those who have brought you pain and forgive yourself in order to grow and move forward.

Today my ordeal allowed me to see and understand myself more clearly and the fact that none of us are perfect. It has kept me humble and increased my desire to forgive more, love harder and stronger than before. It reminds me that I am nothing without God in my life and that I need the Holy Spirit to direct and guide me.

ALEJANDRO CANADY

Alejandro Rey Canady, Sr. is a retired Manager for the State of California Department of Motor Vehicles and is currently a Bus Operator at AC Transit. During his career with the State of California, he has managed and mentored new and seasoned employees and received several service awards during his tenure there.

His hobbies are bodybuilding, writing, and singing. He has previously performed cover songs with several local groups and performed live at various venues in the San Francisco Bay Area.

In Alejandro's story, you will understand his desire to find his identity and where he came from while searching for his biological father. His goal in life is to encourage individuals to never give up, to strive and rise above their past; and become the best they can be in their present. To connect with Alejandro, email him at AlejandroCanady@gmail.com.

NEW BEGINNINGS

Djuna Yvette Hunter

"You made all the delicate, inner parts of my body and knit me together in my mother's womb." Psalm 139:13 (NLT)

My story began in Salisbury, North Carolina in 1964. Anna, age 17, met and fell in love with Wilson, age 19. Anna was introduced to Wilson through one of her close friends Liz, her next-door neighbor. After courting for a while, Wilson made a decision that it was time for him to enlist in the United States Air Force. This would mean he would have to move away to attend basic training and then transfer to his home base in Maryland.

After a few weeks of Wilson moving to Maryland, Anna found out that she was pregnant. How was she going to explain to Wilson that they were going to be parents? How would he take the news? Surprisingly, he took the news well and, in the winter of 1965, Anna gave birth to a beautiful baby girl, Djuna (DW-A-NA).

After my parents settled into marriage and parenthood and had a second daughter, their relationship began to fail and ended in divorce. Between the ages of four and 13 years of age, I had no contact with my birth father. As far as I knew, his where-a-bouts were unknown which meant there were no visitations. I would not see my father again until I was 13 years old.

Not having a father in my life led me down a path of self-destruction and into a life of promiscuity, drugs, and alcohol. No child would understand how traumatic of an event this would become. For a daughter to lose a father figure could be the start of a downward spiral into low self-esteem, a lack of self-worth, and looking for love in all the wrong places. The lack of a father in a daughter's life can play a role in whom she chooses to love.

Another form of trauma I experienced was at the age of six years old. My sister Kimberly passed away at the age of 17 months on December 24, 1971. These events would be seared in my memory for years leaving many unanswered questions.

These traumatic events have one thing in common: abandonment. Abandonment is the act or instance of leaving a person or thing permanently and completely. Two very important people in my life had left me. I felt alone. Many times, abandoning someone is not something that is done intentionally; but when it does happen, it plays a huge part in a child's cognitive, social, physical, and emotional development especially during the formative years, which are between the ages of 0-8. Abandonment is something I have struggled with on many occasions in my life. Realizing that Jesus has been a constant in my life has helped me to deal with my abandonment issues and cling to the promise that *"He will never leave us nor forsake us"* (Hebrews 13:5 NLT). When I came to really understand this, it was so comforting to me.

After years of many broken hearts, I had finally found someone who treated me completely different than all the rest of the guys I had dated. Most of the guys I had gone out with I thought were really interested in me but in reality, they were not. They were only interested in one thing and I wanted so desperately to be loved that I gave myself away. I had finally found that missing piece in my life that I longed for – to be loved and nurtured.

It was a Friday night and Lacy introduced me to Niko, a guy she was interested in. I must admit when I first saw Niko, he really caught my eye. After a few weeks, Lacy had moved on and decided to call it quits with Niko. In March 1989, Niko and I became I inseparable. In February 1990, Niko asked me to marry him. Prior to our engagement, Niko enlisted in the United States Marine Corp Reserves, but before he left, we decided we would date exclusively while he went away to Tennessee for technical school.

Things went well and once he returned from tech school, we dated long distance for about a year before getting married on April 20, 1990. Niko traveled to Maryland every weekend to see me before and after our wedding. It was an exciting time. We were so happy and in love! Our first few months of marriage Niko lived in North Carolina and worked on base as a Jet Mechanic. I lived in Maryland and finished working in Washington DC while he looked for housing. In May of 1992, our first son was born at the local Naval Hospital.

In July 1990, I moved to North Carolina and one month later, Saddam Hussein invaded Kuwait. Niko's squadron was activated and off they went to the Persian Gulf. Neither of us was prepared for a deployment, but we really did not have a choice. What was supposed to be two months of cold weather training turned out to be an eight-month deployment. Niko returned home on April 18, 1991, two days before our one-year wedding anniversary.

The first year of our marriage was difficult being away from family, living in a strange town, and knowing only one person. I did, however, attend a small church down the street, joined a few weeks later and gave my life to Christ on September 30, 1990. That was the best decision I made in my life. It was the holidays, and I was headed to Maryland. I called an old friend to meet for drinks, who I dated for a year and a half before I met Niko. Our relationship was not strained, but Zach was afraid of getting too close, he got scared so he broke off the relationship with me.

We met for drinks and one thing led to another, but I really did not think anything of our being intimate with one another at that time. The decision I made that night would change the entire trajectory of my marriage. As crazy as it will sound to those of you reading this, no thought went into what transpired. The question of right from wrong never crossed my mind. The enemy had me completely deceived.

It was not until I was lying in bed the next morning that I looked over at the bookshelf in my mom's house and saw "The Book." I randomly opened it to Psalm 51, read the chapter and realized that my actions that night were awful. I had committed the sin of adultery. The Holy Spirit led me to that book. I was a new believer and did not understand any of this until much later in my walk with Christ.

It sounds unbelievable I know, but this is exactly what and how it happened. I was never able to explain this to Niko, but God knew and because of this I had peace. I prayerfully repented and asked forgiveness right away, never to repeat the sin of adultery again. Some years had passed, and Niko decided to question me about things and basically, he tricked me into admitting that I had an affair. At that point, he admitted to having an affair as well.

I felt such relief to finally have this monkey of guilt off my back. Now, we could forgive each other and move on with our lives. The two of us, now new believers in Christ, could have a clean slate and move on…NOT. I quickly forgave but was not forgiven so easily and lived with the constant reminder of my sin. The emotional and mental abuse that I went through was awful. I thought it was just me not being a good enough wife or mother, so I kept praying to God asking Him to help me to do better. I would go to Bible study trying to learn so I could be and do better.

I came to understand in the latter years of my marriage that I had been enduring emotional, mental, verbal, and spiritual abuse. But wait, I was always taught that abuse was physical? This in fact, is not true. Words create deeper scars and wounds and are much harder to heal even though they are unseen. It takes time and sometimes many years of therapy to work through the trauma of those types of abuses. I did not want to live. I was suicidal!

Knowing I had done nothing wrong, I would defend myself repeatedly until I heard the Lord say to me, "I have won the battles, let Me fight them for you; I am your Defender." From then on, I stopped fighting for myself. There came a time when I would not speak to men at church because I would be accused of having affairs. As the leaders of a marriage Bible study, I became resentful and bitter living with a man who was not being the godly man he professed to be while leading others, especially his own family. Consequently, when we separated and divorced people were totally shocked. But no one sees what goes on behind closed doors and the abuser only lets you see what they want you to see outside the four walls of their home.

Hiding behind a smile, I was hurting deep inside for myself and my children. We went on to have two more children, a son in 1995 and a daughter in 1999. In 2005 and 2009 we also adopted two little girls from China. These were very exciting times in my life. I wanted so deeply for my marriage to work. I continued to pray for God to help me but at the same time I wanted to be out of this miserable place of existence. I loved this man and I felt sorry for him, but I hated him for the things he would do and say to me; for the pain he had put me through. I think back to the sleepless nights talking in circles about the same things over and over again with no resolution. I wanted to get off the merry-go-round.

This went on for many years. Incidents of being kept in the bathroom or bedroom until I would confess to something I had not done. My anxiety would shoot through the roof and because of the trauma, I would be in a constant state of fight or flight. Fight or Flight is where my adrenaline would be stuck in a state of hypervigilance; unable to relax. I find myself living there even today. So, until I could leave the situation I would always be thinking of a way of escape. I would place my car keys nearby so I could leave the house if I needed to because the conversations were so intense, and I was tired of being accused of something I had not done.

Many times, when this happens it is because the accuser is doing the very thing they are accusing you of doing. I later found out that he had been unfaithful to me on many occasions in our marriage even up until the very end.

Five years into the marriage I wanted to leave but I did not know how I could leave. What would our families say? I did not have a job or money. Also, in God's Word it says that He hates divorce and I believed this. While God hates divorce, He hates what divorce does to families mostly. I do not believe that He would have wanted me or anyone else to endure the pain that abuse causes. Did not Christ come to set the captive free?

There were red flags while we were dating that I did not see. One instance was when Niko came for a visit, but I did not hear him at the door. I let him in, and he rushed into my room looking to find another man there with me and had a few choice words to say. Right away there was a jealous spirit, but I did not see it. On a few other occasions he would call me awful names. Names I had never heard before much less ever been called them and other fits of jealous rage. I dismissed them because I was so blinded by love.

It was not until after we had separated in 2018, after 28 years of marriage, that I realized I was a victim of domestic violence. Forming those words out of my mouth was extremely hard but it had become a reality for me. I had lived a life under such control that I did not know who I was any more. Mother and wife was all I knew. The control was so bad that I felt smothered and that only heightened my anxiety. As I began to study psychology at Liberty University in 2017, I came to understand that I was also suffering from Narcissistic Abuse (NA).

I had to educate myself on the topic, learn the behavior, and manage the way I would respond and handle each situation differently in order not to react. Narcissists love to get a reaction out of you. The more you come to understand the topic of Narcissistic Personality Disorder the healthier you will become as a person. Under this type of abuse, you are being manipulated and controlled. In public they wear a mask to make themselves look a certain way, but behind closed doors they are totally different – Dr. Jekyll and Mr. Hyde.

My life was altered in many ways. My mind was always on high alert wondering what my abuser's next words or actions towards me or my family would be. Would he be kind or accusatory? I was in a constant state of deep internal pain. There are many other traits that a narcissist portrays such as selfishness, self-absorption, lack of empathy, the inability to love, an excessive need for attention, and admiration just to name a few.

Once I began to navigate how to live in this environment, to my surprise, my husband left our home in 2018. Although I was shocked, it was hard to unlearn a lot of what was seared into my mind. Part of this is called trauma bonding – an emotional attachment which is developed out of a repeated cycle of abuse. This is something I knew nothing about until I did my research. For example, these are continual thoughts about what would happen if I did this or that or what would happen if I did not come home when I said I would.

Once the separation happened and we came upon the new year of 2020, I asked God what my word of the year should be, and He told me "new beginnings." Never in a million years could I have ever imagined what my life would be. After thirty-two years, I am no longer in an unhealthy relationship. I have moved into my first home and am on a journey discovering who I am. God has given me that new beginning He promised me, and it has continued until today. He has been with me every step of the way through my journey, and I am forever grateful.

Although I faced many dark days of depression that I never thought I would come out of and there were many days I wanted to give up, it was God Who helped me to see that my life was worth living because I am worth fighting for.

"I am grateful for the new beginnings that God has given me and will continue to give me in the very near future! He makes all things beautiful in its time. Also, he has put eternity into man's heart. Yet so that he cannot find out what God has done from the beginning to the end." (Ecclesiastes 3:11 NLT)

I have learned from my ordeal that I am strong and resilient, but most of all that God has been an ever-constant presence in my life. He has been with me, He has given me the strength to go on, and He has carried me through some of the darkest days of my life.

With the pieces of my life that have been restored, I am helping others to see their worth, to love themselves, to find their voice, to value who they are as an individual, and to take their power back.

It is my hope that my story will help others see that there is a light at the end of the tunnel after domestic violence. Having Jesus Christ as my Lord and Savior was my anchor. Without Him, I would have never made it. There is joy on the other side of the sadness and loneliness that you feel while going through the darkness. Hold onto Jesus! He is faithful and will fight the battles for you... just trust Him completely.

Wow! Today, I have been given a new life and a new beginning! A life I never dreamt I would ever have. It has given me my life back in so many ways. I have found myself again – the person I had lost over 25 years ago. This ordeal has shaped me into a person who now loves herself. It has given me the freedom to openly share how God has restored my life and given me beauty for ashes. He makes everything beautiful in its time.

DJUNA YVETTE HUNTER

Djuna Yvette Hunter is a single mother of five; born in Washington, DC, and raised in Southern Maryland; Charles County. A survivor of Developmental Trauma Disorder and Domestic Violence, Djuna continues to work through the healing process of Complex Post Traumatic Stress Disorder (C-PTSD), Trauma Bonding, Emotional, Verbal, Mental, Spiritual, Financial and Covert Narcissistic Abuse as well as Abandonment Trauma, procrastination and fear; a product of trauma. Djuna also suffers from High Functioning Anxiety and Clinical Depression.

Through her decades of counseling, it was not until the past few years that Djuna has come to understand who she IS as a person and how to take her power back; to stand up and not be afraid. She learned that she was more than a wife, a mom, a sister and a friend; that she IS someone to be valued; someone who has a voice and IS someone whose opinion does matter! During this journey called life, she has come to love herself unconditionally and understands that God has been with her all along. Her journey has brought her to a place of discovering happiness, joy, laughter and peace. She is looking forward to new beginnings!

An advocate for domestic violence victims and survivors, Djuna looks forward to mentoring other women and young women back to life. To get in touch with Djuna, she can be reached at Irelandgrl65@gmail.com and on the following social media platforms: Djuna's Heart on Facebook Messenger, @Pureheart6501 on Instagram and @DjunasHeart on Twitter.

PRESSING TOWARDS MY PURPOSE

Deborah M. Robinson

"Not as though I had already attained, either were already perfect; but I follow after, if that I may apprehend that for which also I am apprehended of Christ Jesus. Brethren, I count not myself to have apprehended: but this one thing I do, forgetting those things which are behind, and reaching forth unto those things which are behind, and reaching forth unto those things which are before, I press toward the mark for the prize of the high calling of God in Christ Jesus." (Philippians 3:12-14 KJV)

When life throws all kinds of curve balls, you might ask yourself, "what do I do now?" Who shall I call? I often asked myself, "do I give up or will I fight back?" America is living in challenging times where there is civil unrest, racism, Covid- 19 disease has spread globally, at-risk youth, and crime is at an all-time high, and the government has failed the people of America. Where do I turn to for safety and peace? The Bible declares, *"let us not lean to our own understanding"* … Trust in the Lord during difficulty.

My story starts when I was a high school graduate just finishing school. I grew up in a hardworking middle-class home with five brothers and one sister. Raised by two very religious parents, my

97

father was Catholic, and mother was Baptist. Two totally different religious belief systems but, yet they believed that marriage works. Divorce was not an option in the Jackson family. Through the good and the bad you stayed married no matter what the bad held. There were times where money was limited, utilities might have been cut off and our family did not have a lot but there was plenty of love to go around. You did not hear of a lot of crime. The family grew up in a close-knit neighborhood where everyone knew everyone. Love was the rule of thumb. Neighbors were a village when you have love as a priority in your life. Mom always had the Sunday dinners, holiday gathering, and outdoor picnics. I can remember on Saturday washing hair and pressing combs with the red jar of royal crown hair dressing. When you walked into the house you can smell the hot comb. Mom was preparing us for church the night before. She would have our clothes laid out and baths were taken. The smell of collard greens, ham, and macaroni and cheese was cooked on Saturday so when you came home from church on Sunday you knew that meal was ready to eat and that it was family time. It was that foundation that made me the person that I am. It was the values that my parents instilled in my brothers and sisters. The struggle with the flesh and spirit is where I questioned, "where do I go from here?" Do I continue to believe in the Catholic Church where my family attended, or do I go in a different direction? I was hungry for something new.

While still living at home with my parents, my older brother came home and said to me "I want to take you to visit a church." Well, of course, I said, "okay, let's go!" I always looked up to my brother, so I trusted his judgment. He takes me into this church one day and it was somewhat of a surprise. When I looked around, there was loud music and people dancing all around with loud stomping sounds. My first thought was 'where in the world has he taken me?' I could not believe all of this was going on in a church. But one thing that stuck with me was the love and the joy everyone had. I did not realize that it was the Holy Spirit that made everyone happy like that. I had never been in a Pentecostal church before. The strange language that was spoken in tongues made me afraid. I quickly realized that it was something that I wanted, and it was not at my church. Curious about what I saw, I began to visit on a regular basis. The more I visited, the connection grew as I came to know my brothers and sisters in Christ. The mothers in Zion were the gatekeepers and when they hugged you, believe me you felt loved. When they put their eyes on you. they could see right through you. I said within myself, "this place is really genuine and real." Church just was not church as usual. This place was like being in heaven. When we prayed on Friday nights it was all night. We brought our pillows and stayed up all night long. When morning came, we went to breakfast. On weeknights, Bible study was power packed, and you did not leave the church until 1:00 o'clock in the morning. At that time, being a teenager, I did not have a car, so the bus was my option to get home. My family did not understand what was keeping me in church that long because as a Catholic I only stayed for one hour. There was a love of God that was like no other's touch. When the Spirit hit you, it would move you from place to place. When you got it, nothing felt like it! It simply could not be explained. The choir was anointed and when songs were sung the building shook. I could not wait to see what was going to happen in the next service. Mind you, the church was in Northwest, Washington, D.C. in the worst neighborhood. I witnessed drug addicts, prostitutes, and homosexuals walk into that church and get touched by God. No one was judged for their lifestyle. They were treated with honor, respect and shown the love of God.

After knowing how that touch felt and the love of God, I just wanted to tell everyone. The spirit of evangelism came on me and I started witnessing and inviting friends and family to church. I am so glad I had a chance to experience such a wonderful and powerful renewing in my life. It was like a rebirth and renewal of the spirit. God was truly my lifeline in such a world whereas a youth, I needed direction and answers. The church soon became my family and it taught me to be loyal to what was heard and seen. No one made me go or put demands on me to attend church. The urgency to keep going came from the Holy Spirit. Following the Holy Spirit will lead you to truth.

Later, as a teenager I moved from mom and dad's home and brought my first apartment. Although living on your own as single person loneliness becomes apparent and before you know it you start inviting the wrong friends to your space. The flesh starts talking to you even when you are all alone. I was still attending church on Sundays, weekly Bible studies, and 4:00 am prayer. What is important to know for our single, divorced, and widowed individuals is addressing topics such as fleshly desires that plague you when joining the church – when coming to God. Do not hide it under the rug but have conversations to help them to overcome the sexual desires that plague their flesh. I encourage you to have conversations with young adults and do not condemn them for having struggles in the flesh; but take the time to speak with them so that they can understand how God feels about the struggle and how they can have the victory over the flesh. Sex is not a disease, and the church and community leaders cannot sweep it under the rug. If the church, as a Body, does not take the time to explain the weaknesses of the flesh, our youth will learn about it from other sources which are not good.

The first voices of instruction and explanation that our children should hear are those of their parents and positive, spirit-filled leaders. Leaders should speak into our lives in such a way that aligns with the Word of God so that whatever is spoken over you will manifest and give God the glory. We have to discern the voices that are spoken over us. It will carry us into our destiny. It must be addressed with our young people. An especially troubling trend to acknowledge is the desire for the same sex relationships. As a church leader, minster, teacher, we must move from traditional church to educating this generation. The more we educate we can pass on a rich legacy of wealthy information that will be passed on for generations to come. Many churches have youth groups that mentor, guide, and instruct the next generation to know who they are in God and what God expects from them as they grow in the natural and in the spirit.

Having a lack of knowledge and understanding about relationships has cost our society a high divorce rate. The church is the voice for relationships. Jesus performed the first wedding in Cana. Adam and Eve was the first couple in the Book of Genesis. Praying and asking God for a mate is not enough. If the mate walked up to us, would we know if that was him/her or are we for looking something as the old saying says, "tall, dark, and handsome." If we are not careful and we do not listen to what the Holy Spirit is saying to us, that person could cost us a lifetime of pain and agony. Do not get me wrong, maybe it could have worked but having knowledge as to what to do when it comes your way can make your discernment sharper and you have your emotions left in tack. My advice to you as ordained leader is to wait on the Lord. When you wait you will see that person spiritually, mentally, emotionally, and physically. It takes years to learn a person's behavior. Learn to be a friend first before you fall in love with the flesh.

Usually, time will tell through trials and tribulations if that person is for you. Many people come to church looking for a mate but find out later it was a different outcome. What looks good might not be for you. Everyone wants to be loved because it feels goods. But you want the lasting results of a mate who will be there forever. The agape love of God is the unconditional love. The shape of the person will fade away. Their hair will eventually turn gray. Love will never fade. It will always be there, and it will be a driving force to continue.

Let me end this chapter by saying everything comes with a manual. When we drive a car, we cannot drive until we read the manual. Read the manual, which is the Word of God. He is the one Who created us and made us new creatures in Him. And when we read, we will get instructions downloaded from Him on the whole man. Take my advice, it took me three marriages to get it right. It does not stop there; it requires hard work to continue the respect, honor, and push for a mature marriage. A perfect couple is just two imperfect people that continue to lean on God's shoulder. The most important advice to engaged and married couples is to see the person as God sees them. Your love will continue to sharpen, and forgiveness will always be available. Just as God gives us grace, we lend that same grace to our partners.

In my conclusion men and women of God, you must press into your victorious life with God. He has a life created for us and has written it out with your name on it. Continue to press forward to the high calling God has for you. His Word is true and cannot lie. Listening to the Holy Spirit has allowed me to share my journey with others so that they will experience deliverance that will be a testimony and will become a catalyst to set friends and family free from the bondage of sin and pain. My journey is to see all man and women set free and walking into their purpose.

What I learned from my ordeal is that God has a plan for His people. He wants to bless His people with the best. I have learned that when you have a personal relationship with God, you learn His attributes, which includes the working of the Holy Spirit. God has taught me patience, trust, and believing in Him. When I learned to trust God, this gave me the strength not to depend on people to love me. I have learned to love myself and not to look for others to validate me.

The vision of my ministry is to tell others through writing articles, books, magazines, and songs that marriage can work. This will encourage others to follow a Godly plan and not allow yourself to get sidetracked. My motto is to "stay focused on your journey." God will grant you your heart's desire if you just be obedient to His Word. God is always concerned about our concerns. The person that

I have been shaped into today is spiritually strong and ready to impart truth in my friends and family.

Leading by example is important. Many people read books, but do not see good examples of marriage working today. People are looking for love and hope in relationships. God is in the business of manufacturing relationships and marriages. If it worked in the Bible it, should definitely work for us today.

Continue to press toward your purpose and do not give up on your plan. God has the keys that unlock the door to your purpose. My ordeal has made me successful in every area of my life. God has chosen me to Pastor His sheep. He has given me honor and not shame. God's children do not have to walk around with their heads hanging down. God has erased all the hurt, pain, and suffering that I have experienced through being in toxic relationships. God has blessed me with a godly husband who loves me for me. I am proud to say he has changed my demeanor and gave me a new address. Allow God to make you and mold you into His image and likeness. Continue to give God the praise and never be ashamed of your testimony.

DEBORAH M. ROBINSON

Deborah Marie Robinson is a wife, mother, grandmother, speaker, teacher, drug counselor, certified license chaplain, business owner, and ordained licensed Pastor. In 1998 Dr. Robinson started Restoration Outreach Ministries, LLC. ROM is a non-profit organization and was incorporated as a church on February 12, 1998, and received it's 501(c)3 on March 22, 1999.

Dr. Robinson has taught at woman conferences, workshops, and she mentors students in District of Columbia schools. She has taught in the correctional systems in Maryland, Florida, and Virginia. Many have received the Lord in revivals, chapel services, and Bible study. Dr. Robinson continues to live by the scripture Jeremiah 29:11 *"I know the plans I have for you declares the Lord, plans to prosper you and not to harm you plans to give you a hope and a future"* (NIV).

To speak with Dr. Robinson in her ministry endeavors, contact her on:

Linkedin.com/DeborahRobinson;
Facebook/RestorationOutreachMinistries

OVERCOMING GOD'S FINAL DECISION:
YOUR HEALING AND HOPE

Hartford J. Hough

In the study of human growth and development, we learn that death is a part of life. It would almost seem contradictory that the cessation of life can also be a part of it. The thought of death frightens a lot of people. So much so they do not even want to talk about it. It is the casual conversation that immediately shifts to a discourse of humor or excitement. How can anyone find a safe space to discuss the finality of one's life and not be moved to another emotional state of being? While we examine death as being "the end," we must clearly adjust our perspective and attitude towards this subject. It is when we look closely into the meaning of death, as it pertains to human life, that we can see it is not really a scary topic or anything to be "afraid of" as we walk the continuity of our human experience. What is death? By definition, it is the end of a life of a person or organism. But is it really? Our optics of death have included so many images that when we hear it, we think of funerals, cemeteries, families coming together, flowers and memorial services. For many, these images can be haunting and terribly traumatic, following them for years until they are faced with it again. Death, as some would say, is that "unwelcome visitor" that comes when we least expect it, and always takes someone or something away from us. We have to come to a different resolve when talking about or dealing with God's final decision. I say God's final decision because He is the giver of life and ultimately the One Who will take life away. I came to understand this at a very early age, and the understanding of this concept has given me new perspective in facing it.

I have known death since I was child, and my first introduction to it changed my world and me to this present day. My mother passed away when I was twelve years old. I have said this before, and it bears repeating, no child should experience the death of his parent(s) at such a young age. Our mothers and fathers are our world. They are the first people we come to know and learn to trust. They are also the first ones that we learn to love as we grow and develop in their care. So, when they are taken away by death, we feel that trust is broken, it shatters our world. I loved my mother intensely. I was so attached to her that where she went, I wanted to go. At times I was often told to stay back and mind my place as a child. I was not supposed to be in "grown folks' business." I did not care about what those people said. She was my mother. Not only was I going to be by her side, but I felt the need to protect her. In the years that God gave me time and space with my mother, I grew to know her. Her personality. Her likes and dislikes. Her wonderful taste. I also acquired one of her greatest traits, her kindness to just about anyone which showed me who she really was. It was the smile she gave me when I gleefully ran around her as a little boy who wanted to play with his mother. Or it was that stern sound in her voice when she knew she had to discipline me when I was not always on my best behavior. Mothers are the first women we as men know, so that bond is indeed strong between a mother and her son. Our relationship was so simple, and this caused me to want to be with her all the time. Whether we took a walk to the store, a ride on the subway or our Sunday morning time at church. Yes, my mother was the woman I grew to love and trust. Sadly, my father was not in the picture as much, but I had the undying love and support from my mother's parents, my mother's twin sister, and my mother's oldest sister, an aunt who also loved me unconditionally. I also had an uncle (mom's youngest brother), we were not as emotionally attached, but he was still my family. Being surrounded by this much love and support, who would have seen my world shattered in a matter of a few years that I would never quite come to understand.

I remember the first time death came to our house. It was the day Dr. Martin Luther King, Jr died. I was three years old, and I recall all the older people (that is what they were to me) crying uncontrollably. I know there was a great sadness in the air. Outside, people were yelling, screaming, and crying. This visitor that had come was not a welcome presence. Losing my mother threw me into a myriad of emotions. She could not be gone. My mother was so young, beautiful, and full of life. How could she be dead at thirty-five? No one really took the time to explain to me what death was and as a child I was left to try and figure it out on my own. This task should never be given to a child. The first time I went to a funeral, I was always told the person was "sleeping." So, I figured at some point they would wake up. Not only did they not wake up, but they were taken to a place far away from our house. It was like a park, with flowers, grass, and trees. The grounds were beautiful. We took the person there, stayed awhile and then we left them there. I would never see that person again. Who was this awful visitor that came, made people sad, and then took them away forever? It just did not seem right.

As the years passed, I grew to hate death. I also became fearful of it. What if it came back one day for me? What was I going to do about it? These are the questions that plagued my mind for years from childhood to adult. As I grew older, I came to understand more about what death was and what it was not. I also came to my faith and knowing God in a very real and personal way. Knowing Him has made the concept of death much clearer and how I could move on in life and not fear its presence or even a conversation about it. Death was not my enemy. The real enemy was fear. We all fear what we do not know. This is where the connection between my faith and conquering fear made the confrontation with death more tolerable.

Losing a loved one is never easy. It never has been, and it never will be. As we continue in this human experience called life, we will soon come to understand that death has value. Now this may seem strange saying that from the onset and elicit the question "what value is there in someone dying?" The value is not in the person dying, but in death itself. You see, from the moment we were born into these frail, mortal shells that we call our bodies, each has a time limit on it. Each day we live we are moving closer to an appointment with death. It is an inevitable fact. We are going to die. What we must realize is that death is not the end, but the beginning. This is where hope must take root in your heart and mind. What is hope? It is a feeling of expectation and desire for a certain thing to happen. As a man of faith, I have come to understand that this body is temporal and what lives on the inside of us, our soul, lives forever. My hope is that when someone dies, they will transition from this life, into life eternal...Returning to the Creator in right relationship and spending eternity with Him. Death then simply becomes a door they must pass through. While we will undoubtedly miss the person, and there will be a period of mourning, we must have hope that we will see our loved one again. That is the hope that will cause you to look up, appreciate and celebrate the life of the one who passed, and move forward as life will go on.

I have also come to understand the concept of death as it pertains to other living organisms that encompass our lives. In particular, the loss of a pet. Death, being the visitor that will once again come, is not unexpected, but it is also not to be feared. Losing a pet, in many instances, is a death in the family. For those of us who love and cherish our beloved animal companions, their life has just as much significance, and when we lose them, the pain is equally felt. When we have these amazing creatures in our lives, we also learn that their life span will be much shorter than ours in the human experience. Their little bodies will age so much faster, and unfortunately, the presence of death will come sooner. Letting them go is that bitter pill none of us wants to take. When we look at our precious animal companion, we want to give to them a portion of what they gave to us. Most animals suffer from some form of a disease or body function shutdown that will end their lives and anyone with any degree of humanity should never want another living creature to suffer. If you are faced with that decision, you are not only ending their suffering, but giving them the most beautiful act of love as they gave to you. It has always been my prayer that God would let them pass naturally. For the pet parent who comes to this juncture in their life, it is that love that will carry you through the loss of your animal companion and keep the treasured memories in your heart as you face the days without them.

The absence of your pet will linger days, months, and years after they are gone. As you seek to find solace, trusting in the memories of your heart will guide you through and bring you to a better understanding of the loss…Remembering the day you brought your precious animal companion home for the first time. The love you felt for them and the bond you formed. The emotional depth that this loving creature took you to when you looked into their eyes. You played with their ears. You allowed them to lick your face, and you smiled. It is those memories that will evoke the best of what you shared with them and give rise to the hope within. Love is the most powerful force in the universe, and it will never die. Knowing that God loves you so much that He created you in His own image, and then entrusts you to care for one of His creations with time and space in your journey of life. It is that glorious hope that the foundation of our faith is built upon. God, in His infinite wisdom, would not allow you to be blessed to love and care for a pet and not bring that love back to you when their life is over. Here is where death is not the finality, but the commencement. Know that all the love, joy, happiness, and goodness you felt here will be eternal nuggets of bliss as you are reunited with the loved one that never really went away. They were simply waiting at the door for your turn to come through. Once you come through, what an overwhelming joy that will be felt by everyone.

As we go through life, there will be many experiences that shape and mold us into the person we were actually meant to be. We also know there will be some experiences that have a traumatic effect on our lives. We must see those as valuable life lessons. One may ask, what can you learn from the death of a loved one. Death is hard enough as it is. How can there be a lesson there? It really is a lesson to be learned. I learned not to fear death. I came to understand it at an early age, and when the realization that it is just as much a part of life, I gained a whole new perspective on death and how to approach it. When I lost my mother, I thought my world was destroyed. I loved my mother and the thought of her being gone was unbearable, even for a twelve-year-old. As I moved into puberty and young adulthood, I learned that life does indeed go on. You must go on with it. You accept the truth that another individual died, not you. You still have life and must move forward. That is the key right there – move forward. Anything less than that, and sadly you make the person's passing seem in vain. Whether you are a child or an adult, death can shatter you emotionally, physically, and spiritually. The hope, in the midst of it, is that you can pick up those pieces and live. I did. I learned that my best years were yet ahead of me and if I was going to see them, I had to LIVE!

I will always love my mother and treasure her memory to this day. Even so, when I lost my beloved animal companions, there was a hole that only God's grace and love could fill. He did. I channeled that energy into positive means, where I speak to individuals who have had loss. I can empathize with love and compassion. I can be sensitive to their situation, and learn to understand pieces of their process, and know when to speak and when to be silent. I can also offer this counsel to those who have lost their pets.

When the devastation of loss has come, there is a kindred kindness and place that only someone who has experienced this will understand. Most people do not try to understand. I do. I have to because I want to see others healed as I have healed. Remember, life moves forward.

It is my prayer that as I share my experiences with death, one would not be frightened or turned away. Death is something we all are going to have to experience. It is an inevitable fact of life. I want those who read my story to understand that I still have my moments in dealing with the loss. The holidays, birthdays, family gatherings, are just a few of those moments when the rush of emotions hit you so hard. While it may be hard, it also causes you to remember. In remembering, that stirs up treasured memories that light the heart and bring a smile to your face. Losing the people and animals I have had has made me a stronger, sensitive, resilient, and deeply compassionate man who will always extend himself to the needs of another and bring them up from what may seem a shattered experience known as death.

HARTFORD J. HOUGH

Hartford J. Hough is an award-winning baker, chef, and cake designer. He is also a member of the IACP (International Association of Culinary Professionals) as well as a member of The Humane Society and The ASPCA. A man who loves God, he is also a passionate animal advocate and a man with an assignment to show forth the glory of God in all of who He is and has created. He is an author, speaker, radio show host and current minister in training. He is the author of the national best-selling book, *"The Fur Beneath My Wings: Our Relationship with Animals and The Valuable Lessons They Teach Us,"* and the forthcoming work of non-fiction, *"Ginger: The Journey of Two Hearts, One Human, One Animal"* a literary work dedicated to the life of his beloved animal companion and the transformative power animals possess in the lives of their human counterparts as a manifestation of God's creative power.

His work within the homeless community also gave way to seeing that not only must we be concerned about our fellow human beings, but everything that God has created and understanding its purpose here on earth. He continues to serve in his church and within various homeless organizations in and around the Bay Area of San

Francisco. A member of New Hope Christian Fellowship, he is also establishing himself as a servant in ministry and teacher of God's Word. Hartford firmly believes in the power of God's love and has not only experienced it but is determined to share that love with a lost and dying world, bringing them back into right relationship with God. You can follow Hartford on facebook.com/Hartford Hough and on his website www.thefurbeneathmywings.com. *"The righteous care for the needs of their animals but the kindest acts of the wicked are cruel."* (Proverbs 12:10)

PERSERVERANCE THROUGH DARKNESS

Lakisha Jenkins

I will first start by saying I am blessed to have survived my past life experiences. I have endured several, some of which were self-inflicted and others that were out of my control. Through each challenge I have managed to trust God for better moments. At times, I came close to giving up but somehow it was necessary to find enough strength and faith to keep going. Enduring so much pain, heartbreak after heartbreak, disappointment, losses, and even moments of abandonment was rough for me. The emotions I have felt caused me to feel numb inside. As a young adult struggling with so many issues in which others did not understand and without a support system, caused me to feel helpless at times. Through my struggles of loneliness, depression, PTSD and anxiety over the years, I had lost sight of things and my choices in life began to affect me. For several years, I lived a life of emptiness and unhappiness.

Early on in life I battled repeated stages of not knowing or understanding how to love me. This opened the door of unhealthy choices and cycles of continuous self-inflicted pain. In my early twenties, I faced so many circumstances that left me completely damaged inside, searching for love. All that mattered at that time was being able to numb my pain and fill the empty void I was carrying. I stayed in toxic and dysfunctional relationships due to my insecurities. Several years later I recognized the effects of choosing to cope this way.

Learning to love me first has been one of the best decisions I've ever made. My beginning stage was not easy at all. It took me to feel tired of the repeated cycles pain. Pain from childhood experiences, feeling hurt by men, impacted by repeated losses in life and most of all feeling incomplete. Getting through this phase took courage. I had to learn for once how to take control of my life and my decisions. Implementing change was necessary. I needed to feel I could do this. Most of all, I needed to know I could dedicate the effort it took to make it happen.

Beginning mid-2013, I had faced a painful break-up that became my starting point of recognizing it was time to form change. Deep down inside I was dealing with so much past regret. One of my goals was to get to a place where I could move beyond the feelings of failure and unworthiness. During this process, the challenge of loneliness was the hardest. I was so used to having a man to fill my empty void inside. There were times during this period that I found myself giving in to my weakness, only to strive harder to resist temptation. This was definitely the first sign of growth for me. Over time and seeing that I was capable of doing better, I began to crave emotions of hope and belief in myself for once. This felt great and with all my previous obstacles, setbacks, and strongholds, I could feel a sense of change happening.

After getting to a point where I could begin to understand myself and now begin to properly love myself, I faced the most devasting time of my life. Keyshaun, my 14-year-old son was murdered by someone I was dating as the result of domestic violence. This incident took place on October 15, 2015. Every bit of self-love I had gained was gone. I found myself in a place of not knowing how to survive. At times, I felt unworthy of surviving. This was the darkest place ever for me. Dealing with so many emotions regarding self-sabotage was unbearable. With my case being high profile and, in the media, I struggled with shame, guilt, embarrassment and carried some of the responsibility. The thing that hurt the most about losing my son was to accept that I was willing to render help to this person (the perpetrator, my son's murderer) and in return lost my son who was not willing to settle for disrespect. Realizing that just because I was willing to love me and love others, they [he] also needed to commit to love themselves as well. Mentally, I was lost because of this feeling and things became extremely difficult moving forward. My thought process was off. I found myself going through a period of isolation not wanting to deal with anybody. At times being scared to leave my home in fear of being noticed. Being judged by what people thought of me was overwhelming. For months, I felt clueless and hopeless not knowing how to deal with such feelings. I did not have a healthy outlet at the time, so I found myself heading back down a damaging road with men during my moments of grief. Daily, I craved and prayed for an outlet for my pain. Mentally, I was not capable of thinking straight so I depended on my old ways of managing things. I went back to what was familiar. It brought a strange sense of relief. I continued this road for several months before acknowledging the inner damage I was doing to myself.

One day after taking time to examine the things I was allowing and choosing to cope through my pain, I realized I had to do better. Somehow, I begin to reflect on my self-value even in the midst of loss and grief. I instantly made the choice to push through no matter what. Each day I promised myself and Keyshaun I would do whatever it took to progress. Making that promise was easy but committing myself to it was not. This process took courage, a new mindset, and again complete belief in myself. I also had to be willing to do something different as well. That difference for me was therapy. Therapy was not completely new to me. Keyshaun and I attended counseling together before he passed away. I knew some of the benefits therapy could produce. It was helpful with the circumstances I endured as a single mother raising an at-risk youth. Our previous therapy brought relief and change into our home before Keyshaun passed away. That is what made my grief process so hard. We had just begun to move past the difficult times and be happy again.

Choosing therapy, this time around, was a lifelong commitment. So many emotions were built up inside of me which I had no way of understanding. Even though I was open to therapy, I lacked how to move forward. This time around putting the pieces together was so much harder than any situation I had ever faced before. I was clueless this time. Therapy became helpful with finding a sense of direction. I continued therapy for over a year. I was amazed to see how my choices in men connected with my past traumatic experiences. This was a very serious stage for me. This is where my point of healing was first introduced. Therapy became my reason to hold myself accountable. It is one thing to not know, but when you do know it is time to implement some type of change, change became my top priority.

Another choice that helped me along the way was asking God to give me insight and strength to move beyond my pain. Prayer became a daily routine for me. One day after feeling so lost I kneeled at the bottom of my bed, praying, and crying for strength to see some form of light again. Even though I was trying my best, I still felt lost at times. It was the thoughts of holding on to the little self-value I had left and continuing to challenge myself to recap reasons to survive that kept me alive. Suicide was never an option for me. As time progressed, I began to notice changes in myself and that made me push even harder.

Months after continuous therapy, my mental state became less challenging. I was now able to sense just a piece of that self -love aspect again. I began to feel motivated again. Going through therapy was the beginning of my breakthrough. Over my time being in therapy, I had two wonderful therapists. My first one moved on to a bigger field and my second decided to relocate. This presented a huge problem for me. I was now faced with needing to find a new therapist. Previously struggling with certain separation issues in my life to now building relationships with therapists that were about to come to an end, caused a sense of anxiety for me. Before my therapy ended completely, I was able to adapt with necessary coping skills and positive outlets to help with finding balance when therapy came to an end. I prepped myself as much as possible to get to a point when I felt I would be able to function on my own. It was not my wish to be in therapy for the rest of my life.

In 2016, I felt the need to form a way of self-encouragement for myself as well as others. Self-therapy was a top priority for me. Forming my own ministry became a major thought. In the beginning of gaining this desire, I had no name but insisted on proceeding anyway. Motivated as ever, I started to do encouraging videos in my bedroom. Speaking whatever came to mind and what I felt could help others. Upon pushing through my own personal challenges, God confirmed that I my ministry should be called SELF LOVE MINISTRY. Each day I was striving to achieve better love for myself. In the beginning fear was a major setback. The more I showed up, purpose started to form around me. The more that I committed myself fully, God revealed how my testimony could help so many people. Today, it has been almost five years since I have started my ministry. Today, Self Love Ministry is still impacting people's lives and growing strong.

Pushing through any dark moment requires hope...Hope to survive the circumstance you are facing. Change is also necessary, which requires you to gain a new mindset. Change brings new desires, confidence, determination, and motivation. Giving up should never be an option for anyone. You owe yourself the chance to recover. Our strongholds are meant to keep us bound and stuck from progressing. Do not remain comfortable in an unhealthy or unhappy place. Move forward, be willing to acknowledge the undealt with issues, the generational curses, or the past trauma. Dedicate the effort needed to get you back together. Just do not give up!

Had I given up on any of my life's struggles, I would not be here today to share my testimony as a survivor. I would have missed the biggest blessing God could have ever given me. Another chance to be enjoy motherhood. My youngest son, D'Andre, born September 12, 2017 has been a huge impact in my recovery process. Losing Keyshaun caused so much self-sabotage. I did not feel I was worthy of ever becoming a mom again. D'Andre has given me that push I needed to realize – despite how we feel about ourselves – if God sees fit, He will grant the necessary blessings upon your life.

The best way to describe my current journey is enjoying my self-discovery mode. This entire process started years ago with learning how to first love myself unconditionally, then becoming strong enough to maneuver through a series of hurt, pain, disappointment, feelings of abandonment and even loneliness; and later, becoming capable of addressing my unresolved issues and pursuing change. I have faced several episodes of grief over the years. My grandfather (1997), father (1997), husband (2009) and most recent my 14-year-old son (2015). Each of which impacted my self-esteem, self-love, self-worth, and most of all, formed insecurities but I managed to recover and be a living example for others.

Today my main focus is to continue my path of healing. With recently deciding to put and keep God first, my path is progressing better. My self-confidence has taken off. I am in such a new and exciting place right now. I encourage every reader to commit to their required healing process. Healing is necessary if you want to defeat the many strongholds over your life. Healing allows you to release the brokenness and damage inside. Commit yourself to the process needed. Always remember that the process will be continuous so you must stay ready at all times. Each challenge you face will try to discourage your strength but remember WITH GOD ALL THINGS ARE POSSIBLE!!!

Looking back at where I started, I would say my life has transformed for the better. My journey of dealing with grief has been quite challenging and it has also introduced a level of determination like never before. I am now able to mentally challenge myself to not let depression take over during the rough moments. Thinking positive and positioning myself around positivity truly helps me to balance when things become hard to manage. I feel more capable of encouraging others who may be having a hard time dealing with grief.

I am extremely grateful and feel blessed to have made it thus far through all my challenges. I live each day to encourage, inspire and uplift those who may be struggling and need some reassurance that all things are possible with God's help. Had it not been for the one decision to include Him within my healing process, I am not sure how my life would be today. I was in a place that felt so dark with no hope of every seeing any light in my life again. It was that repeated voice in my head that kept saying "Kisha you are valuable" that constantly challenged me to shift my thinking and find a way to push like never before. This is why I have committed myself to forever live for God and be the example others need to see. Life feels amazing to have overcome my darkest moment and enjoying living my life for God to the fullest.

My hope for anyone who reads about my life experiences is that the words "never give up" will repeatedly alarm in their head, constantly challenging them to first do the work within to achieve the level of change desired, always remembering to include God and trust that He can bring them out of any situation. I also pray that whoever reads about my journey is able to gain a greater view of change to defeat any past strongholds, creating a mindset to W.I.N (walk in newness). If you believe that you can, then you will. Speak positive things into yourself. Aim to let go of any negativity and watch how your actions begin to line up with your mindset. Believe it, speak it, and eventually you will walk into it.

I will end my chapter by reflecting on the level of growth I have endured since the passing of my 14-year-old son. Overall, I am much more stronger and wiser than before. I am cautious of my decisions and my environment. I take more time to think before I react. I have managed to let go of fear and self-doubt. I have been able to gain the courage to challenge myself in ways I have never imagined. And most importantly, I have chosen to keep God first in order to achieve the absolute best that's meant for me. It is only because of God and through His guidance that I was able to finish strong despite my past challenges. The level of strength I have been able to gain has positioned me in a place of determination and perseverance which I have never had. I am committed to defeating every storm that comes my way. All I know, after these last six years, is to push… "pray until something happens," believing and knowing that God has complete control of whatever the end may be. With His guidance, I am protected and with His guidance I am fully assured that I am covered.

LAKISHA JENKINS

Lakisha Jenkins, a South Carolina native who resides in Maryland, is the founder of Self Love Ministry which she formed following the loss of her son in 2015 as a result of domestic violence. She has also battled the loss of her husband in 2009 as well. Lakisha has pushed through her pain with a great desire to help others by becoming a self-love coach, a motivational speaker, and an author of two books. She has battled depression, low self-esteem, and a low self-image due to the traumas that she has faced throughout her life. However, she has been able to tap into her inner strength and find healing in God and, also in supporting other women who have faced similar life altering experiences.

Lakisha's overall goal is to inspire, uplift and encourage women to love themselves in spite of what they have been through and to see themselves as victorious, not victims. She is transparent, truthful, and compassionate towards women and the many challenges that they face and has made it her life's work to help heal them.

You can connect with her through Self Love Ministry on:

Facebook: Smileyface Kisha
Instagram: @coachkjenkins
YT- Coachk Jenkins
Email: lovingme1st_selflove@yahoo.com
Website: www.selfloveministry.net
Contact phone number: 1(800) 583-9121

THE HURT THAT BIRTHED

Kacey Cunningham

"My flesh and my heart may fail, but God is the strength and the portion of my heart forever." (Psalms 73:26)

You want to know the curse of growing up in a small city? Everyone thinks that they know your story! The parts that they do not know, they fabricate as they go along. Here is the part that they got right: I am one half of identical twins, raised by a single mother, while my father was in and out of prison, divorced mother of one to my beautiful daughter Jazelle Kathleen, all the while being faithful and remaining active in my church family. Stay with me! I am going somewhere with this. See now this is where my story seems to get quite confusing.

Shortly after my divorce in June 2018, I thought I had hit the jackpot when I met the man whom I thought was a "God-fearing," charming, and great man. This is the man who approached me like a gentleman. He respectfully asked me out on a date. He opened car doors for me. He held doors for me. On our second date he brought me a blanket in case I caught a chill in the movie theatre. We seemed to like the same things. We talked and discussed so much about things we both had been through. We would take walks in the park

133

and go out of town. He seemed to understand me. As we continued to see each other, he seemed to love me, to actually care for my daughter and me. He even went and discussed our relationship with my Pastor. Whew, that was a tough one. But soon the love turned into manipulation and anger. His studying of God's Word turned into manipulation and anger.

Our first argument, I had a panic attack. I could hardly breathe. I found out that he was still entertaining other woman via phone, social media, and even in person, some even being out of town. I had never had a man yell, belittle, or talk to me the way he did. But he knew that. He threw my laptop and some other personal belongings outside. I told myself that night that it was over. The next day he came to me with a new laptop and empty promises, and I took him back. For months I kept telling myself and he always did little things to reassure me that "the good outweighed the bad," that "all couples argued." Then there came the promises that he would stop drinking and continue going to therapy. I even started going with him…then he stopped.

"Kacey, I thought you were smarter than that." They would say, "Kacey, wouldn't allow him to do that to her. She is stronger than that. So those rumors just can't be true." Yes! I thought I was smarter; I thought I was stronger than that, too. Without a doubt, I had family and friends to come to my aid, telling me to leave. Ironically, I shunned them, turned away from them, still trying to personify a happy relationship, all the while I was busy helping others I could not see or better yet would not see that I was the one who needed help. His family became my family. I treated them as such, and I loved them dearly. My family, however, came with claws and they were not letting up, which created an even bigger barrier between me and them. I never thought you could actually lose family without someone passing away, but I did. I lost valuable and meaningful friendships. I pushed them away and they did not want to stand by and watch what I was succumbing myself to. My mother wanted what I wanted, allowing me to make a mistake and then learn from it, never leaving my side as a watchful eye on me and her granddaughter.

Was everyday a bad day? No. But the bad days were so detrimental and extreme that they overshadowed the good days. Yes! My biggest insecurity at the time and it had been for a while, was the constant comparison between my twin sister and me. We were twin sisters, but for some reason I always heard that she looked better than me, she dressed better than me, that she was more girly than I was. That had taken its toll on me from my early years until this day. He knew that. Throughout our relationship he made it a priority to instill in me that I was too good to be in anyone's shadow. I needed to be in the forefront because he had plans for us. If I uttered a word that led him to believe that I even thought that someone was better than me or prettier than me, I knew an argument was coming.

Our last big argument on July 4, 2019, was because he said that I was taking up for my sister, that I always took up for her and that he could not see why I could not see that she was not better than me. My head is spinning as I write this. That night I was hit in the face, knocked to the ground, and dragged outside of his house by my legs. The police were called that night and I lied to the police officer and told him that he never touched me.

He looked at me and said, "Ma'am, I can tell by looking at you, that he hit you in your left eye." Even after that, I still went back. Even with a bruised face, I talked myself into believing that he did not do it. I lied for him, I covered for him. His go to lines were, "I don't remember doing that," and "you always *cover* your man." Within time, the manipulation made it so challenging that I felt like I could not go to or depend on anyone but him, especially when he knew I was in need and what my weaknesses were. But he also knew my strengths. He knew he had a good woman. He knew I was a believer in God. He knew I was business savvy. He knew I could cook. His plan was for me to do all of that…with him, but God had another plan that He wanted me to open my eyes to see.

It was one afternoon in August 2019 and we were at a restaurant discussing a great business adventure we were about to start – one that he knew I wanted so badly. We had already established a nonprofit organization, that ironically was growing with members, and that confused me even more. But more and more I pondered on our past history – the arguments, the tears, the manipulation, the hurt. See, I knew that if this business deal went through, I knew the next thing was that he was going to propose to me. That's when I had what we like to call a "come to Jesus meeting" with myself. That very moment in that restaurant, God asked me, "Do you want this for you and your daughter the rest of your life?" I simply said. "No, I don't!" and I walked away, scared, lonely, hurt, broken, and confused.

Jazelle, my daughter? She loves her mother. Unfortunately, some situations within that relationship took me away from her. A chronic ectopic pregnancy, which destroyed my left fallopian tube, made it impossible to properly care for a 3-year-old the way a mother should. I will never allow myself to take "me" away from her again.

J. Kathleen Catering and Events LLC was birthed from someone thinking that he had all the power simply because he told me I had none. It was me finally realizing that my daughter, Jazelle, was all the earthly power I needed. My daughter and I have been growing TOGETHER, hand-in-hand! Our business thrived from the start and it is still thriving.

The hurt I endured birthed ME! Can you learn from hurt? Can you grow from hurt? Can you forgive hurt? Yes, to all of the above. Through Christ, I was able to turn my hurt into blessings…repeated blessings. This birth did not happen overnight. I endured many,

many months of indecisiveness, emotional, mental, and spiritual brokenness, and many months of labor pains. I had to undo his manipulations. I had to unlearn some of what he taught me. I had to right many wrongs. I had to repair many broken relationships.

I leave you with some lessons that life's hurts have taught me:

1. Never say what you will or will not do or go through.
2. Portraying strength does not make you strong
3. You can overcome anything that you are faced with
4. Not every man is the same.
5. The hard part is not forgiving them; the hard part is forgiving yourself
6. You will love again

There is no greater feeling after so much hurt than to have your 5-year-old daughter look at you and say, "Mama, we are happy!"

I look at the "Kacey" I was. The mother I was. The daughter I was. The sister I was…and daily I realize that there is always room for improvement! As a child growing up, I'd roll my eyes, shrug my shoulders, suck my teeth, sometimes all three (smile) when my mother would give instructions or reprimand me. But, as I sit and relish in moments such as this, I find myself saying, "Mama was right!" I see why she kept me in church every Sunday, every second service, Bible Study on Wednesday, every church meeting. I see why my grandfather would allow me sit in the living room with him and listen to conversations when Pastors and Deacons would stop by the house. Why? Because they were instilling within my brain, my memory, and my heart, life lessons that I did not see nor understand back then...BUT NOW!

Since "the end," I have understood more and more the song lyrics, "God is the joy and the strength of my life. He moves all pain misery and strife." Some think that once you walk away that the battle is over. No, Ma'am. No, Sir. The battle has just started. The difference is that you are now walking in His will, so you will not have to fight alone. Satan's plans never change; just whom he uses to try to implement his plan. People can be harsh, especially when your mistakes have been made public. Will the harshness end? No, Ma'am. No, Sir. Will it always affect you? No, Ma'am. No, Sir. Someone else's interpretation of you, what they think of you, will not stop God from blessing you. Once we realize what our power is, we can use it effectively and for good.

Today, I live my life unapologetically. I create my own happiness. I refuse to settle. I will not crawl through life scared or with fear. I will dance through life exhaling every blessing God throws my way. Restoration within myself allows me to spread a little bit of joy, a little bit of happiness to the next person. It allows me to breathe in and breathe out knowing that every day I tried my best to be the best mother, daughter, Christian, I could be.

If you don't take anything else from my story, understand this, YOU CAN RISE FROM ANYTHING and YOUR PEACE IS EVERYTHING! When I am troubled, hurt, or saddened, I get into the WORD and I surround myself with those whom I KNOW are for me! Your past is not a period. It is a comma! Something will come after it!

KACEY CUNNINGHAM

Kacey Cunningham is a Christian, mother, daughter, sister, friend, and motivator from Danville, Virginia. She is an Administrative Assistant for Focus Point Mental Health, LLC, a Small Business Owner of J Kathleen's Catering & Events, LLC, a Certified Business Consultant, and a Notary Public. Her daughter, Jazelle Kathleen, is her inspiration and her driving force.

Kacey is a strong advocate for her community, its potential, and its growth. She motivates others to believe in themselves and their dreams regardless of current circumstances and/or environment. She lives by the motto: "Some of life's hardest and toughest battles are some of life's biggest blessings!" Her favorite scripture is Psalms 73:26, *"My flesh and my heart may fail, but God is the strength of my heart and my portion forever."*

Her goal is to empower those who feel that mistakes cannot be turned around, who feel that hurt can't be healed, and who feel that dreams can't be attained. She wants to instill in others that once you realize and "use your power," ANYTHING IS POSSIBLE. Her social media handles are:

Facebook: @jkathleenscatering & @useyourpower Instagram: @jkathleenscateringandevents.

Her 'Use Your Power" podcast is coming soon. Live life faithful, fearless and unapologetically!

About the Visionary

Michele Irby Johnson

Michele Irby Johnson is a retired, disabled Veteran who is an Energetic Motivational and Transformational Speaker and Trainer as well as a Certified Life Coach who is a much sought-after voice who serves the Abused, Women, Non-Profits, Family and Education, Veterans, and Faith-Based communities through her unique style that reaches deep into the hearts and lives of those longing for transformation, elevation, inspiration, and empowerment. Michele has a great love for seeing people's lives changed. Through speaking, training, coaching, and mentoring, she gets joy in developing and elevating people to a place of greatness, seeing them reach their goals, and helping them to see their tomorrow through the lens of who they were called to be in this world.

Michele's gift as a transformation architect has afforded her the opportunity to serve surrounding regions through speaking, preaching, retreats, conferences, and teaching workshops and seminars on Domestic Violence to such groups as educators, medical personnel, clergy, women's ministries, and youth alike. Her capacity has allowed her travel and serve in such areas as Maryland,

Washington, DC, Virginia, North Carolina, Alabama, Tennessee, Florida, Texas, Guam, Southwest Asia, and Africa.

As a survivor of Domestic Violence and an advocate against Domestic Violence, Michele penned her first literary work entitled *"Love's TKO: A Testimony of Abuse, Victory and Healing,"* which shares her experiences as a victim of a love gone bad through domestic violence. To continue her love for writing and reaching others through this gift, she has penned her second literary work entitled *"Grace For Your Journey: Sermons of Survival in the Wilderness."* She is a best-selling Co-Author of the anthology *"Women Inspiring Nations Volume 3: I'm Still Standing."* She has several other literary works in progress that she believes will prove beneficial to reader from personal, emotional, and spiritual perspectives.

As an educator, Michele serves as an Adjunct Professor at a local university, teaching Health & Wellness classes to undergraduate students; and teaching Counseling Women and Domestic Violence Crisis Counseling (two courses she wrote) to graduate students. She is also passionate about helping people be administratively prepared for the inevitability of death. As a bereavement liaison and consultant, she has written and delivers Estate Planning webinars and workshops to specialized groups, organizations, churches, families, and individuals. She firmly believes that having such affairs in order is a great display of a legacy of love one can leave behind for their families. Her vision is to provide peace of mind for your future.

Michele holds five degrees: Master of Arts in Counseling (Crisis Response and Trauma); Master of Arts in Human Resource Development; a Bachelor of Science in the field of Human Resource Management; as well as two Associates Degrees from the Community College of the Air Force: One in Education and Training and the other in Social Services. She retired from the USAF after 26 years of combined dedicated military service with the 113th DC Air National Guard at Andrews Air Force Base. Michele is affiliated with Veterans-N-Transition, Transformation Academy, Apostolic Grace Evangelistic Fellowship, Speaker Hub, Fair Consulting, Association of Christians in Leadership (Advisor), Black Speakers Network, and Elevation Entourage to name a few. She also hosts her own Virtual Talk Show: *"Life Matters with Michele,"* which airs weekly on Facebook LIVE and is also posted on her YouTube Channel Life Matters with Michele TV Official.

In April 2020, Michele started the Grace Point Radio Broadcast with her husband, Apostle Shaun P. Johnson, Sr. on the DMV Power Gospel Radio Network. She now broadcasts **Grace Point** on its own YouTube Channel Grace Point TV Official and on Sensational Sounds Radio weekly, both platforms taking to heart the necessity to spread the Gospel to all the world in hopes of introducing the lost to Jesus Christ, reclaiming the backslider, and to minister comfort, strength, encouragement, and healing to the brokenhearted.

With this literary work, Michele and her husband have launched a self-publishing consulting business that helps authors to fulfill their dream of being published. They offer design services, project management, editorial services, and more.

In her spare time, Michele enjoys watching HGTV, the Golden Girls, and any type of Cold Case, Forensic Files, or crime shows and spending time with her husband, Shaun P. Johnson, Sr. Together, they have three sons, one daughter, and one grandson.

Connect with Michele
Facebook/LinkedIn: Michele Irby Johnson
Instagram: Michele.irby.75
www.iam-mij.com
www.optimumpvs.com
www.onekingdompublishing.com
www.livingbygraceministries.org
www.kingdomcbi.org
YouTube: Grace Point TV Official
YouTube: Life Matters with Michele TV Official

Other Literary Works by the Visionary

Love's TKO:
A Testimony of Abuse, Victory and Healing

Grace for Your Journey:
Sermons of Survival in the Wilderness

Contributing Author in the following literary work:

Women Inspiring Nations Volume 3:
I'm Still Standing

Made in the USA
Columbia, SC
24 June 2021

40417071R00096